Tihon Hieromonk
THE ARCHBISHOP

THE
ARCHBISHOP

TIHON HIEROMONK

I. Costiş Mihai (Romanian translation)
II. Hluşcu Gabriela (English translation)
III. Savatie Baştovoi (Foreword)

Foreword

he *Archbishop* is a book that provokes. Written at the beginning of the 20th century, the book continues to be a cry against the ecclesiastical conformity.

The author, Hieromonk Tihon, of whom we have no information, is unsatisfied with the lukewarm atmosphere that reigns within the Church. He devises an ideal shepherd in the person of the main character of the book – the Archbishop – who strives to bring back the apostolic spirit to priests and believers. Nothing prevents us from believing that this Archbishop may have existed for real and that he, himself, wrote this book.

The Archbishop is a literary work, a fiction novel, not a treaty of ecclesiology. This should not come as a surprise to us. The Russians are sensitive people who prefer listening to a hymn about God or reading a poem than studying the dogmatics. Perhaps, for this reason, they have not offered the world creators of philosophical systems, but rather great writers and artists.

The Lives of the Saints, written by Saint Dimitri of Rostov whom many criticize for the abundance of idyllicism and literature, is a representation of the way the Russian people understand Orthodoxy. In my opinion, Father Tihon's book seems to be part of the same style, with its main purpose being not to serve certain norms and prejudices, but to touch the heart of people.

Although on a particular level, the book is meant to be a program of spiritual commitment, it should be read as an interesting and realistic chronicle, maybe too honest at times, about the ecclesial life. The author is a great writer, nourished in the heart of the great Russian Literature. The characters are vivid, honest, not invented. The book is a pleasant read and cannot be forgotten.

14

Savatie Baştovoi

I

———⟡⟢⟣⟡———

ather Paul was sitting on the ship deck, drinking. The bottle on the table in front of him was half empty. He had sipped glass after glass, at short intervals, without tasting the food at all. He was drinking obstinately, defiantly, smirking to himself and emphasizing on purpose the nature of his occupation: "Behold all of you, Orthodox brothers, admire your shepherd!"

The generic term *Orthodox* was used by Father Paul to refer to all the passengers on the ship, lots of whom were already throwing cautious looks towards the table of the priest, and carefully searching with the tail of their eyes for the captain of the vessel. A few mothers pulled the sleeves of the children who were frolicking on deck and, by using different and more delicate pretexts, took them away from the troubling priest. Clearly understanding the attitude of the public towards his figure, the Father did not intend to stop. On the contrary, he tried to show his complete indifference in every way. But most of all, he wanted to be scornful to a fellow priest who was walking on the deck, giving the impression of admiring the beautifulness of the scenery. The imposing outfit, the definite pacing, the dainty motions of this person disgusted him in particular. Father Paul could not distinguish his face, for the priest had kept himself at a distance and had only flashed glances over the shoulders.

"And with what does he show off, I wonder?" thought Father Paul to himself. "He is a priest just like me only that, perhaps, he ministers in a town, and I bet his income is around two thousand rubles. With a pay like that, anyone can look all high and mighty. Bleah... I'd really like to see him walking in my shoes. Look at him... He can almost pass for a bishop!" The Father's heart turned bitter from these thoughts, and the envy towards his imposing brother grew even more. He picked up the glass and drank it down, then churlishly spat on the floor. He did it so energetically that his hat, which was barely hanging on his head, rolled down to his feet. He had no intention whatsoever of picking it up, instead, he leaned all his weight on the table, fixing his dizzy look on the people around him. He noticed how the priest in question had turned around and had begun approaching him in a calm pacing. Without lifting his eyes, Father Paul pricked up his ears to listen to the soft noise of the footsteps and the rustling of the cassock. The stranger was close. The desire of pulling a practical joke that would place the new-comer in an embarrassing situation overwhelmed him.

16

"Father, hey little Father!" he shouted, giving him a witty look when the priest passed by his table. "Fancy a glass of vodka?"

The priest stopped, quickly fixed his gaze on him and said smiling:

"Thank you brother, but I do not drink."

He then picked up the hat from the floor, straightened it carefully, and took a seat next to Father Paul.

Father Paul hardly expected something like this to happen. He thought he would become the target of a hateful look at least, after which his "sinless" brother would move on, while he, Father Paul, would be laughing behind his back. However, this unexpected behavior of the stranger disarmed him. He felt extremely embarrassed. The thought of having insulted a kind-hearted man intimidated him. In order to minimize his insolence and get rid of the discomfort created in his mind, Father tried to continue the conversation, shifting it from sarcasm to the illogical tone of a groggy man.

17

"Where are you from?" he asked, casting a short glimpse to his new interlocutor.

The guest arranged his cassock, made himself comfortable and, by turning towards Father Paul, he answered with a relaxed and serene voice:

"From far, far away... Behold! I travel, admiring the great Volga. So much wealth here, so much boundlessness! And so much life; if we only count the passenger on the ship! Only by seeing it with your own eyes, you would understand why our people love this river so much; why they mention it in their songs and why they miss it when they are away. It is truly a great river."

"Well, of course, it is!" nodded Father Paul.

Being born and raised on the shores of Volga, Father Paul was proud of the river and loved it like a true inhabitant of the province. The praise coming from the newcomer flattered him. There was no trace of the old hostility anymore, so he started to listen with a growing benevolence.

"You have great wealth here"— continued the guest— "but much sorrow as well. Many tears and despondent worries. Yet, this is not the greatest affliction. I had the opportunity to witness the lives of a small group of people at the outskirts of the country who live far worse than most of our peasants. They only wear rags, eat cornmeal mush or barley bread. At times, even that is hard to obtain. But if you look at them: they're all giants like pine trees. Their walk is sprightly, their appearance is so majestic as if they were not covered in rags but in tunics. One might believe they have no problems or expectations from life and others. Thus, our affliction is neither poverty nor grievance. Our affliction concerns the Russian brother who doesn't know how to endure the hardships of life or the bitterness of its burdens. If they get hold of him, he either arms himself with patience— a strong and lasting patience— or starts to endlessly complain. Usually, he wants to get rid of his problems by repressing, stifling or silencing them. As you are doing it now. The plague has come upon you and instead of confronting and defeating it, you gave in to drinking... And by having done that, you added a bigger burden on top of your previous one."

18

Father Paul was staring at his brother in amazement. "How does he know I drink out of pique?" he thought to himself.

"But look how much strength you have"— said the guest, patting the Father on the back— "and those sturdy shoulders! With them, you can carry not only your burdens but others' as well."

Suddenly, Father Paul adopted a livelier posture. He remembered that the peasants from his home village, his parishioners, often admitted that nobody could compete against him in physical labor.

"And yet another Russian feature," the guest carried on, speaking mostly in his beard. "Calamity strikes the Russian brother, and behold, he ignores it, acting as if he neither hears nor sees anything. He does not care at all if, maybe, someone else suffers from an even greater pain. We like to pour out the vials of our wrath in the open but we fail to notice that, by being so preoccupied with our own troubles, we burden others as well. Like you are doing right now."

"Well, whom am I adding my burdens to right now, may I ask?" wondered Father Paul.

"What do you mean to whom? Behold! You are sitting here drinking and drowning your pain away without noticing that man over there, for instance... See the gentleman sitting on the bench? Earlier, we've passed through a village with a church, so he took off his cap and made a cross sign on himself. As you can see, faith still exists in his heart. Now, tell me, isn't it painful for him to see a shepherd of the Church defiling himself with such occupation?"

Embarrassed, Father Paul looked with the tail of his eyes at the bottle and the glass on the table while his guest discretely called the server to come and take them away. Father Paul did not object but instead tried to justify his behavior somehow.

"Well, as you well noticed, Father, I am drinking out of pique. Great and heavy is my burden."

"You will feel better if you tell me your burden, share it brotherly, and perhaps it won't seem so heavy anymore. A burden shared is a burden halved."

Father Paul had felt on his own the need to put his heart out to this kind Father. The reasons were his gentle face and, especially, his intelligent eyes; serious but sad, and always full of compassion and warmth. People as such take interest in a stranger's suffering out of something more than simple curiosity.

"I've been sentenced to trial," began Father Paul. "I've wedded without documents... The situation was this; a young lad and his girlfriend came to me, asking to be wedded. She was an orphan and so was he. They both worked at a factory and so it happened that the poor couple gave in to the temptation of sin. Still, they wanted everything prepared according to God's law and with His Grace. But yet, another issue; they didn't have any papers! She had lived with one of her aunts but ran away, leaving her papers behind. His papers were expired, so he sent them to be renewed. However, they still hadn't arrived on time. 'No way —I told them— without papers it can't be done!' 'But Father, —they asked me—

20

is it ok to live like this, without God's blessing?', 'This is not my concern—I told them— go back where you came from!'

"But they both stood there, begging me; the bride was crying and the groom had kneeled at my feet... What was I to do? I felt pity for them, so I opened the Church doors and called the couple inside.

"'Well, here's what we're going to do —I told them— you are both of age, that I can see for myself. But both of you must vow in front of God and His Holy Face that you are in no way or form related by blood.' They vowed. So I wedded them: 'May God be with you both...' And I did not charge anything for the service. You could tell they were poor from a mile away. And to prevent this occurrence from reaching the ears of our higher-ups, I didn't record the wedding in any register and only gave them a certification which confirmed that they are indeed husband and wife, and that their marriage is legitimate.

"And that's how everything should have ended. Except that, meanwhile, you see, all kinds of comrades appeared in my life... I had a fight with one of them, the church parson from the neighboring village. He brought my case to the consistory and, according to the custom, they opened a case and trialed me... and so on and so forth. I was sent to the monastery for repentance. But first, I went to the bishop, thinking that, maybe, I could soften him. Yah! He didn't want to even see me! Instead, he sent word through his apprentice: 'Tell that good-for-nothing to not even look me in the eye!' I felt completely offended: 'If it's like that, then tell the bishop that not only will I not go to the monastery, but I won't return to the parish either. Let him appoint whoever he wants in my place!' I turned my back and left.

"And, like that, I left the parish, searching for a private occupation. But who needs a priest *in reserve*? I thought to find a job as a courier, but they didn't want to hire me. Heck! People feel uncomfortable letting a man of the cloth carry heavy sacks of oat on his shoulders...

"So, yes, I am wandering aimlessly here and there. I also thought of going to another diocese, maybe to a different parish, and find a bishop with a kind heart who would understand me. For that, I decided to visit the hierarch from around this place. I heard he is kind...

"But to all intents and purposes, misfortune follows me; he just left! He was appointed in another diocese, and now, a new archbishop is expected to take his place. But what am I going to do if the new one turns out to be all high and mighty too? Wander here and there again? But I have my family at home, waiting for me. Soon, we will have to pinch and scrap... How can I not give in to drinking?"

"I would have done the same thing if I were in your place," said the new-comer, revived. "It is not a priest's responsibility to gather prenuptial documents nor to perfect the papers of the betrothed. Missing papers do not prevent the marriage from receiving the divine blessing nor does Grace descend for the sole reason that papers are in order. Marriage has existed since the first ages of Christianity, since nobody had any notion about birth certificates or registrations.

"However, it would have been a different matter if you would have wedded minors. It would have been a great sin because you would have desecrated The Holy Sacrament of Matrimony. The Grace would not have been present in the Holy Sacrament. It would have been like praying for the good health of a dead man or ministering the Holy Sacrament of Anointing of the Sick on a dead body. By wedding minors, you would have broken the laws of nature. Only people who have reached a certain biological age and maturity can be wedded. Why is that? Because both the laws of nature and the laws of morality belong to God since He established them. Notice the silliness that could have resulted. On one hand, you would have broken God's commandment. On the other, you would have asked for His Grace to do so, in which case, Grace would not have descended, of course. Instead of having performed The Holy Sacrament, you would have defiled it.

"Therefore, you've committed no sin. However, the truth is that, by not respecting the formalities, you have been punished. But I wonder, could not have this sentence be endured, at least for the joy that you have bestowed upon the young couple? I am certain that they were profoundly happy and in deep gratitude."

"Well sure they were! Just a few days ago, I came out on the deck, looking to buy some food. Suddenly, I heard: 'How do you do Father, would you like some apples? Please, take some', 'Why wouldn't I? —I answered— 'How much?', 'I cannot charge you, Father. Here... Take them. Don't you recognize me?' —I looked closer— it's her! The bride with no papers! 'How are you?' I

23

asked her, and she answered full of joy, smiling: 'Thank God, Father! The Lord gave us a child!', 'Well, God bless you all!' I said to her, and she placed the basket full of apples in my arms and nicely asked me to take it. What else was I supposed to do?! I took it! I served apples to the passengers for the rest of the trip."

"Well now, you see? But you started drinking... You must endure the burden by praying harder to God! The prayer strengthens the man and freshens his mind. And a fresh and powerful man will always find a way out no matter the situation. You have strength as well as a loving heart. Do not cripple yourself and do not cripple others... It seems we are approaching our destination. We'll disembark soon... It is my first time here too. I have recently been appointed to minister here. Here's what I propose. Come by my apartment anytime. It is located next to the town Cathedral. We can continue our conversation then and, who knows, maybe come up with new solutions. Now, my apologies, I need to prepare my luggage. See you soon!"

The priest stood up, grabbed Father Paul's hand and brotherly kissed him three times.

"Goodbye," said Father Paul, with timidity in his voice. "Thank you for the words and please, forgive me. I did not expect you to be like this..."

"May God forgive you!" said the other priest, heading towards his cabin.

II

week had passed. Father Paul could not find the courage to ask for an audience with the bishop. He read in the newspapers that the new hierarch had arrived and had already taken up his duties.

"I wonder how he is,"—Father Paul worried— "and if he will receive me or not. What if he sends me back to where I came from?"

At first, he thought it would be better to ask someone who already knew the hierarch before seeking out an audience. He remembered an old colleague from the seminary, Father Gherasim, who lived somewhere on the outskirts of the town. He thought of paying him a visit; perhaps he could find out something, no matter how little. He did not dare to go to the Father he met on the ship – his inborn shyness prevented him: "Sure, he's gentle and humble, with a kind heart; he even picked up my cap from the floor even though I thought he was a conceited guy, but... A town priest is a town priest and I simply cannot barge in" —he looked at his shabby cassock—

"especially like this…". In the end, he decided to go looking for Father Gherasim.

The searches did not last long. As soon as he reached the outskirts of the town, he was guided in the right direction by the first person who showed up in his way– a guy with a vagabond appearance– who even volunteered to accompany him to the house of his old friend. Father Paul noticed that his strange guide was speaking with affection about Father Gherasim.

"Are you one of Father Gherasim's parishioners, by any chance?" asked Father Paul, trying to understand the reason for the guide's respectful attitude.

"No, I don't belong to anyone; I am from the asylum. An *asylum inmate*, that's how they call us now. But everyone around here knows the Father. There now! His apartment. Good bye."

The *asylum inmate* went back on his way while Father Paul knocked on the door in front of him. There was no door bell.

"Come in, who is there?" could be heard from behind the door. "Come inside. It's not locked. Push the door harder."

Father Paul slowly pushed the door open and found himself inside the room. He took a squint and then stopped perplexedly. The walls were empty. Close to one of the walls was the bed. Next to another wall— a wardrobe filled with all kinds of flasks and bottles, a couple of wooden chairs, and an old writing table with a tall stack of books on top. At the table, sitting crooked with a book in his hand, was Father Gherasim. He looked very aged and weakened. Father Paul hardly recognized his colleague from the seminary.

26

Realizing that the one who entered was a priest, Father Gherasim stood up and welcomed him in a friendly manner:

"Come in, please come in, have a seat. Gracious Lord, could this be Pavlusha[1]...?! Dear friend, is it you? What brings you here?"

Father Paul did not know what to answer. He gave him a friendly hug, kissed him three times, after which he let himself fall heavily onto a chair and continued to examine the room. His eyes were searching for something.

"How come... How is this possible... What is the meaning of this?!" Father Paul finally asked. "Is it... Really...?!"

He could not finish his question. Father Gherasim realized that and answered:

"You are probably referring at my bachelor apartment. Go on. You'll find the answers you are looking for. Do you remember how all of you used to call me a lame-duck at the seminary? Actually, you were preaching my troubles since as far back as then. And so it happened. I only had one joy and I buried her. And next to her – my daughter... I live by myself, as you can see; all alone, like a country dunny. But never mind all that, let's not reopen old sores. Better yet, tell me about yourself, for we haven't seen each other in such a long time! How did you end up in our town? And, in general, where do you minister? Do you have a wife? What about children?"

27

---

1 Pavlusha – Pet name for Pavel. The Russian language has pet names for all Russian names. People who are close to one another never use their full official name written in their documents. By calling Father Paul "Pavlusha", Father Gherasim shows his openness and sincerity towards his old friend.

Father Gherasim was firing questions at his old colleague who wasn't in a hurry to answer them.

Father Paul was quietly sitting on the chair. He was remembering now the words of the Father on the ship: "Calamity strikes the Russian brother, and behold, he ignores it, acting as if he neither hears nor sees anything. He does not care at all that, maybe, someone else suffers from an even greater pain." What did his pain mean in comparison to his friend's? He was healthy and had a young and lovely wife. And wasn't he the happiest man in the world when his four children, all of them healthy and playful, would frolic around him, would sit on his lap or would climb his shoulders? Live and rejoice! Father Gherasim had been left with none of these joys anymore... And yet, he kept on living!

28

Father Paul was ashamed of how little goodness he had shown lately. In a few words, but lacking the enthusiasm he had on the ship, he told his old friend the troubles that brought him to the town.

"Do not despair," Father Gherasim encouraged him. "The situation is fixable. We have a new archbishop now, non-conformist enough and, as it seems, he's promising too... Maybe he'll look upon your actions from a different perspective."

"Actually, this is why I came to you; I wanted to know what you think of him."

"What can I say... I only saw him when he was greeted at the Cathedral. Initially, I couldn't really tell what type of man he was, but all I can say is that he seemed to be very original. I haven't seen anyone like him before. In fact, I haven't even heard of anyone alike. The entire town still talks about his *welcoming*. You must have heard it too!"

"No, I didn't get the chance. I've only been here for a week or so."

"He too has been here for a week. Last Friday, I received a telegram saying he would come and that we should greet him. All of our staff gathered in the Cathedral. They put on their church vestments and lit the candelabrum. Some of the townspeople came by as well. His carriage was waiting for him on the pier. Everyone was waiting for the church bells to ring, while discussing all kinds of stuff, mostly about bishops. One of the priests, the more waggish one, said a funny joke. He said it so funny and made the archdeacon, who was standing next to the archbishop's throne, laugh so hard that he fell right on the Throne Seat. So there he was, sitting on the throne, laughing and holding the censer in one hand and the dikerion[2] in the other. The others started laughing at the archdeacon. Because of the laughing and chatting, they failed to notice how two unknown priests entered the altar. Perhaps someone had seen them but didn't pay any attention – as if unknown priests are allowed inside the altar... So they entered and bowed humbly, then prayed and kissed the holy altar. One of them was wearing the Adorned Cross[3].

29

---

2 Dikerion – A two-branched candlestick, symbolizing the divine and human natures in Christ. It is used by an archbishop for blessing during services in the Eastern Orthodox Church.

3 Adorned Cross – In the Russian Church, all priests are bearers of the cross. There are three types of crosses: silver cross, gold cross,

He stepped aside, holding a box that looked like the one in which the Kamilavka[4] was kept; the other started examining the interior of the church. He looked around the altar, after which he opened the small door on the side that lead from the altar to the Room of the Verger[5], and entered the hallway where some of our priests would sometimes go for a smoke. Because a lot of time had passed since we started waiting for the Archbishop, many of the clergy were already gathered there. You could cut the smoke with a knife. So the unknown priest headed straight to them.

"Then, out of nowhere, we saw the carriage coming but the bells were not ringing. What could it mean? We were looking around, while the archdeacon and some of the Fathers went to greet him at the carriage; but there was no sign of the Archbishop! 'He's not here yet'– the archdeacon told us.

"Truth be told; I was a bit afraid. I went to the pier and saw that the ship had arrived an hour earlier than scheduled. 'That's it, I am in trouble,'

30

---

and a cross decorated with precious stones. The author used this detail to point out that the priest who entered was a *protos* (first in rank).

4 Kamilavka – A hat in the form of a rigid cylindrical head covering. The Kamilavka is an item for the head among the clerical clothing worn by Orthodox Christian monastics and clergy. As with most items of Orthodox vestments, the Kamilavka developed from the clothing worn at the imperial court of the Eastern Roman (Byzantine) empire. The Kamilavka is worn during church services.

5 Verger – A small room situated at the side of the Holy Table, specially designed to keep the censer and all other necessary items of the altar. Also, there's a small door in this room through which the priest enters. This explains why the two priests entered the altar without being seen by the believers.

I thought. I asked the captain and he told me there hadn't been any sign of an archbishop on board and that, probably, something must have been confused in the telegram.

"The Fathers have gathered together to decide what to do next. And all this time, the unknown priest, who earlier entered the altar, headed straight to the archbishop's throne. He stepped on the orlets[6] and started to take his cassock out; and that's when we all saw *it* hanging at his chest... The encolpion[7]! His companion had opened the box and had pulled out the bishop's kamilavka. The Father placed the skufia[8] on his head, made the cross sign blessing all of us, and said: 'Peace be with you, dear Fathers and brothers! Thank you for greeting me!'

"So it was, that our Fathers and Brothers, blinking their eyes in amazement, were just standing there, surprised— everything happened so unexpectedly.

"Then Vladika[9] continued: 'There were peaceful times in Russia when the Orthodox faith and its archbishops were glorified with high

31

6 The Orlets – A round carpet with the image of an eagle rising above the church. It is used only in the sermons where the archbishop is present, and only the archbishop has the right to step on it.

7 Encolpion – A medallion bearing a sacred picture worn by archbishops in the Eastern Orthodox Church.

8 Skufia – An item of clerical clothing worn by Orthodox Christian monastics (black) or clergy, sometimes specifically awarded as a mark of honor (red or purple). It is a soft-sided brimless cap whose top may be pointed (Russian style), flat and pleated (Greek style), or flat with raised edges (Romanian style).

9 Vladika – Diminutive term used in the Russian Church by priests and believers for their archbishops.

honors. At the chime of the bells, the entire nation would gather and welcome its hierarchs. Now, it's different. Godliness has strongly diminished amongst the people. As for our intellectuals—they completely seceded from the Church. Tough times await the faithful sons of the Church, its shepherds and its archbishops. It is not the time now to think about vain glory but the time for archbishops to take off their golden miter – the symbol of the glory of Christ– and instead put on crowns of thorns; for today, the Name of God is more blasphemed than it is worshipped!

"Troubled times are upon Russia nowadays: worries are haunting us everywhere; thefts, roguery, crimes. The transgressors of God's laws are restless, growing and spreading with each passing day, with each passing hour. And who shall rise to fight against evil, if not us, the shepherds of the flock of Christ? For we wage war against the dark and powerful kingdom of this age, the malevolent spirits of hell. Thus brothers, let us proceed to this great and heavy battle, for in front of us stands The Greatest Shepherd, our Lord Jesus Christ. You must have Him before your eyes in every moment. You must every minute think of Him. I say this to you since, while gathering to greet the Archbishop, you have forgotten about The Great Unseen Archbishop. Here lies His Holy Throne, but you dare to make all sorts of jokes. Here lies the House of God, the pure and sacred Grace of Christ, and you dare to bring the stench of tobacco in it.

"I do not speak these bitter words of truth to punish you, but I realized how often we look away from the heavenly Archbishop and focus our attention upon the earthly archbishop. Who is the one responsible for this and for many other disorders that we have? It is not the time now to point fingers. The righteous and unrighteous, all of you, come together to the holy work of the fallow ground of Christ. Behold the many things happening now on this ground... The words of the prophet Isaiah come to pass: 'And they shall roam about the lands, hard-pressed and hungry; and it will be that when they shall be hungry, they shall fret themselves, and curse their lord and God.'"

"Vladika spoke many. He spoke beautifully. Towards the end, he asked everybody to pray with him before starting to minister together... It was then when the Fathers came to their senses and went to receive the blessing, to give him a warm welcome, and to congratulate him on his arrival... After that, we ministered a *Te-Deum.* When the service ended, Vladika took out his church vestments, put his cassock back on, and stormed out. The people in the Cathedral tried to help him go down the staircase, but he said: 'Do not worry. I am not pregnant.' He grabbed the Fathers' sleeves and told them: 'Well now, show me where my home is and you, Fathers and Brothers, I expect all of you on Sunday evening for a warm cup of tea.' Yes, the Archbishop is original."

Father Gherasim ended his story. Shortly after, he continued:

"Last Sunday, Vladika ministered in the Cathedral. I went there, mostly to see how he ministers. He ministered beautifully. He has a powerful, very sonorous voice. His presence

33

is imposing, but he looks even better in the archbishop vestments. When he walked out the altar, holding the censer in the church, I couldn't help but admire him. A real kingly posture... Tomorrow he will minister here, at the monastery. Go and see him, if you still wish to do so."

"I thought about it too. I have to see him before seeking an audience. In cases like this, my eyes don't lie. Should I like him – I will ask for an audience. But if not, there is no point in trying then."

The conversions between the two friends was interrupted by a knock on the door.

"Yes, please come in," answered Father Gherasim.

The door opened and a slipshod head appeared from behind it; it was the head of an *asylum inmate* from the vicinity.

"Father, you promised to come to us. Please, don't forget!"

"In a moment," said Father Gherasim, standing up.

"Well, Pavlusha, please forgive me; I must leave you now for there is a *little thing* that requires my presence. You are staying at my place, right? Where are you accommodated? At the hotel?! Why would you, I wonder? Move in with me right now, yes? We will live together until your problem will be sorted out."

"If you allow me to, then I would be most honored," said Father Paul. "But I will return a bit later. Today, it seems, you are a little busy. I'll go to the archbishop first, and afterwards..."

"As you wish. If you want to return later, then so be it. Just return. You can tell me then what the Archbishop said."

The two friends bade farewell. Father Gherasim left accompanied by the person who was waiting behind the door, while Father Paul headed towards his small chamber at the hotel.

III

I t was one in the morning when Father Gherasim, tired and downcast, returned to his bachelor home. *The little thing* he needed to attend to after separating from his old colleague proved to be more than he could chew. They called him too late. Fedotici, an *asylum inmate*, desperately needed the Father's help for his wife who was dying. He could not afford to pay a doctor, but it wasn't necessary; everybody knew that Father Gherasim could tend the sick better than many real doctors. Entering the meager chamber of Fedotici, Father Gherasim realized that the woman was already in her last moments. An hour and a half later, she died. Fedotici, lost and confused, was standing alone in front of the Father. Father Gherasim knew that Fedotici didn't have any close friends, so he rolled the sleeves of his cassock and began preparing the deceased for the funeral. An hour later, with Fedotici's help, the Father managed to place the corpse on the table, under the icons.

"Do not take the pain to your heart, Fedotici. Leave it; somehow, we will manage to live like this," said Father Gherasim at parting. He headed back home, leaving Fedotici all alone with the deceased.

The funeral was scheduled for the next day.

Father Gherasim wanted to rest, but sleep had already abandoned him. The happening with Fedotici had awaken painful memories that were now invading him. His whole life passed in front of his eyes, including images of his childhood that had been long forgotten: the village, the fresh forest air, and the field... his father, also a priest... some drunk peasants fighting in the street, two striplings who fell to blows, an inhuman scream in the neighborhood – a man was *teaching* his wife a lesson. "Oh Lord, will the man be ever satisfied? Why do they fight?" Father Gherasim's mother would ask herself, sighing. And her sigh had been imprinted in the mind of the stripling Gheraska, soon-to-be Father Gherasim.

38

The question tormented him during his pastoral school years. Then later on, with more intensity, at the seminary. Only in his fifth year of seminary did he receive, according to him, a clear answer: *There was not enough love; love for the neighbor and love for God. People have forgotten the Gospel. Christians have long forsaken Christ, but without stopping to call themselves with His Name.*

From that moment on, the young and fiery seminarian Gherasim Ivanovici would not talk about anything else except love. His favorite lectures and readings were those where the heroes kept preaching about love. Also, at that time, he firmly decided to become a priest and dedicate all his strengths to preaching about peace and love. He imagined his future parish to be the poorest in the entire diocese, situated in a far away and long-forgotten hamlet.

Not long after, the Father had to give up the thought of a rural parish for he noticed that the people living in towns were even more miserable. These people were residents of different asylums. They lacked and needed more of what Father Gherasim intended to bring to the villagers. The true kingdom of hate and darkness laid here. So the Father decided to go and fulfill his mission in town, as far away from its center or any other rich parishes as possible. He wanted to find a church close to the outskirts, where all the loafers and tramps would gather.

The seminary years had quickly passed. The Board wanted to send him to the Academy, but he refused. He wanted to engage in real-life work as soon as possible. And thus, his dream came true. Gherasim Ivanovici became Father Gherasim, the parson of a church located on the outskirts of the town.

Enthusiastic, the Father started his work and immediately plunged himself into a feverish activity. His burning preaching about peace and understanding, about love and the righteousness of God, poured down like a river. During the Liturgy, Vespers and all the other services, the words of this eloquent, talented and tireless shepherd echoed in the church. His listeners were exactly as he wanted them to be; many of them lost not only the Image of God, but also their human appearance.

The parish was large but the true faithful were few. The majority of the shanties that were part of his parish were inhabited by the town ruffians whom the Father endeared, and who would only enter the church to find shelter from the rain or to beg for money. The listeners whom he had hoped for did not show up. So he decided to go to them himself. He moved the center of his pastoral activity inside a night asylum, right in the middle of these renegades, and began preaching the evangelical love with more intensity. For days, without sparing his strengths and by making use of the gloomiest colors, he would reveal his listeners all the misery in which they were wallowing; the fetid kingdom of vice, of darkness and hate. He would compare it, for oratorical purposes, with the bright Kingdom of Heaven where the divine Grace, the joy of love and the holy righteousness reigned.

The labor on God's fallow ground had proved to be extremely hard. Yet, the Father would sow relentlessly. However, the fruits did not grow. His listeners did not turn out to be better, not even a little, instead they had cultivated a growing irritation towards the Father. In no time, he was forced to notice an obvious mockery towards his preaching.

Once, he accompanied his wife in town for some domestic requirements. There was nobody at home. Later, when he returned, he found the doors to his apartment crushed and the rooms completely emptied. The thieves took everything they could find. A note, written in an unlettered manner, had been glued on the kitchen window saying:

You preached us a lot about sanctity.
The saints did not own anything.
We wanted you to be like a saint.

The happening did not dishearten the Father too much. He was more terrified by the harshness of the human heart. Despite not fully recovering from the event, he began to preach with even more enthusiasm. "It seems that the place is too rocky," he thought. "It's impossible that people hate their own happiness. They can only be happy by receiving the evangelical preaching."

Very soon after, an event would take place that would radically change the course of Father Gherasim's activity. One night, the Father entered, as usual, in one of the asylums to preach. This time, there were more drunk people than sober among the inhabitants. He stopped next to a vagabond who was lying on the bench, semiconscious, in a pond of his own vomit. He began preaching about drunkenness, pointing towards him. As eloquent and empathetic he was at demonstrating the need for mindfulness, as ruthless and fierce as he was at judging it. He preached a lot. Those present were indifferently listening to him, looking confused at their drunk companion. And one of them, soberer than the rest, who was meaninglessly grinning, hummed: "Well, he died."

At first, Father Gherasim did not understand.

"Who died?" he asked, alarmed. Then he realized...

Something within broke and strongly pressed Father Gherasim's heart. Then it went up and fixed itself in his brain, causing him an unbearable pain. He was confused, staring at the body of the one who had served as an illustrative object for his preaching. He looked at it in tormenting restlessness, fuzzily trying to unravel a mystery that had been left undiscovered until now.

One of the inhabitants rolled the corpse on its back, granting it more the appearance of a dead person. His eyes were open, fixing everybody with their stiff look. His faded stare revealed such horror, such terror, such despair and suffering! The Father had the occasion before to bury people who died of an alcoholic coma, but he had never seen anything like this. Back then, death would leave the mark of absurdity, while now — the mark of an endless suffering. Now, death was spoken by the skinny arms gathered in a spasm, the extremely weak concave chest, barely covered with rags in which— he just noticed— countless worms and insects were swarming.

Father Gherasim covered the nakedness of the corpse, by straightening its rags. His fingers accidentally touched the naked body and he felt something sticky and dirty. He lifted the rags and a strong smell of decay escaped in the air. He then saw that the lower part of the decedent's belly was revealing a homogenous wound from which pus was pouring slowly.

Terrified, he quickly withdrew his hands and, with a cloudy look, he fastened his eyes on the other inhabitants. He could now see all that had been kept hidden from him. He could see the mark of the plague under the rags of these vagabonds. To him, all these hooligans, beggars, alcoholics, thieves and all the poor in the world formed a large wound, a dense *canker* swarming with lice, which had been eroding the human body. "God! What have I done?! These people don't need to be taught; they need to be cleaned, washed, taken care of..."

Since then, Father Gherasim has remained silent. He felt a strong embarrassment because of his previous preaching, especially of the ones about the meaning of the earthly suffering from the perspective of redemption. When the Father analyzed his preaching, he identified himself as standing on a bridge and preaching about the utility of bathing to a man who was drowning, without realizing that the man needed a life vest or a rope instead of his words.

He burnt all his missiology handbooks, all his preaching and teaching books, and began collecting medical books. He enrolled in medical courses at the university, set up a pharmacy at home and, with the same ardor from his preaching, he started curing his parishioners of their numerous physical sufferings. The Father had become the most awaited guest; his presence would be needed everywhere, anytime.

This new beginning in serving the neighbor had costed Father Gherasim dearly. After just one month, while curing a man of typhus, the Father himself contracted the disease. His healthy body had survived but his wife, the one who took care of him during his illness, did not make it. Shortly after, he also buried his only daughter.

It's said that the blood of fallen soldiers gives new strength to the survivors that continue the fight. The same way the death of his wife and daughter had functioned upon the Father. In the past, Father Gherasim could hardly be found at home, but now, he would only show up at his house to grab some medicine or to steal a few hours of sleep at night. Not only did he leave his home, but he also left his church. He found spending hours worshiping at the pulpit to be useless while, outside the church walls, the air was filled with moans which nobody could hear; each minute and even each second was necessary to snatch someone from the jaws of death. Often times, while incensing in front of the icons, the Father felt a feeling of reproach growing in his heart. It was against the silent inhabitants of the sky for they seemed to be indifferent to the boiling darkness of humanity's pain of which Father Gherasim, in person, was the center.

And so the bells tolled lesser and the church doors were rarely opened. A thick layer of dust had covered the white garments of the icons.

After ministering the service as quickly as possible, Father Gherasim would hurry up to his sufferers. Their faces would joyfully lighten each time they would see him come. But year after year, Father Gherasim felt that his life was more and more devoid of the inner satisfaction he was hoping to achieve. His own life was becoming more and more difficult and burdensome.

He was curing his patients with a success that inspired optimism, and where medicine proved to be helpless even for the most skillful doctors, Father Gherasim would abandon medication and would surround the sick with so much care and attention, that even the ones dying would bless him with the same gratitude like the one who would get healthy.

His success did not make him happy, though. The more useful his help was, the higher grew the demand for it. While one patient would get better, three other would need his *attention*. He would get one person out of poverty, while other five would suddenly take his place. People from all over the eparchy would come and bring their troubles and pains to him, so the Father realized that, eventually, this torrent was going to drown him too. This thought terrified him. And from that terror, he ended up with a crooked back; his arms had dropped and his hair turned gray.

His heart was filled with an even greater horror when he witnessed the human rottenness in all its fullness. He had seen but a small part of it before; the tip on top, no more than the human eye can normally perceive. By revealing their wounds and pains to him, these people had also opened their hearts.

45

Oh God! Father Gherasim would find so much stench whenever he'd manage to take off the invisible rags used to cover from stranger eyes the people's wounds and the diseases of their soul! He understood now that, for instance, the old women beggar whom he sometimes graciously called one of *his defenders of God*, would beg for money not just to end her hunger. He knew that from what she managed to collect, she would only keep a part of it. With the rest, she would buy vodka and God knows what goodies to lure some guttersnipe who, at the end of the *workday,* would agree to satisfy her beastly lust in exchange for some gastronomic pleasures.

He then learned about the role of the stray adolescents from the asylums who, for a few kopecks[10], would accept to sleep with anybody. In time, many other things had been discovered to Father Gherasim, for people would not spare one another; together with their own sins, they would reveal the sins of their neighbors too, airing their dirty laundry in front of him.

Father Gherasim had found out from the stories of these fallen brings about all the human meanness that lurked in the lower as well as the upper classes of society. But because of them, his heart turned cold, his will broke and his soul froze.

Weight heavy as the plumb had collapsed on his soul, preventing him from continuing his preaching with the same intensity. He started dragging his miserable existence in a silent latency until that weight would crush him entirely. If he had made a few acquaintances among the town dwellers in his good times, now, Father Gherasim had definitively isolated himself into his shell and could rarely be spotted at special events. To the town clergy, Father Gherasim seemed to be a little off the edge.

Before, when his strength did not entirely desert him, he would ask for help from the people who were willing to offer it. He would often visit the previous archbishop, until his sick, bothersome, incomprehensible words started to annoy his superiors. So the Father ceased to disturb them. He stopped expecting help anymore.

For that matter, his behavior did not change too much. He continued to visit the sick, to

---

10 Kopecks – A Russian monetary unit equal to one hundredth of a ruble.

look after the ones from the asylums, to cure alcoholics, to wash the infected, and to bury the ones who had died. But he was doing all this mechanically, like a routine. He did not invest any new ideas in his activity and, later on, he even stopped meditating about his actions.

After wandering through the *parish* all day long, Father Gherasim would hurry home at nightfall to sleep as soon as possible, so his thoughts would not torment him. His attempts were not always successful. During the long winter nights, when the blizzard showed its fierce teeth in the streets, the blistering cold would burst into his room and chased the heat away. Father Gherasim would wake up because the cold would penetrate his bones. He could not sleep anymore afterwards. The sleep would flee away and the thoughts would invade his mind. The howling of the wind, the roaring of the storm, the darkness of the night would stir up his numb imagination. Everything that filled his days would come alive at night, taking different shapes of nightmares. Sick, blind, cripples, skinflints, beggars, drunkards, alive and dead, would flash right in front of his eyes, forming an endless line of human faces. They were moaning, crying, laughing hysterically, stinking unbearably, losing their shape and merging into a huge, purulent and fetid *canker*; in the same *canker* that Father Gherasim had seen for the first time there, at the asylum, on top of the dead drunkard, when he was preaching about the utility of abstinence to the inmates.

The *canker* was growing, expanding, gaining gigantic proportions, and it would crawl towards

47

Father Gherasim. Then, he would jump out of his bed, shaking with terror. After wiping the cold sweat from his forehead, he would walk across the room for the rest of the night, until the break of dawn chased away the darkness together with all the hallucinations that tortured him. And so the days passed, one after another, and life had somehow avoided Father Gherasim. He would view it with the eyes of a spectator who stares impassively at the continuously changing background.

He would feel totally indifferent, even towards significant events of the clergy life, such as the appointmentof the new Archbishop. He went at the Cathedral and greeted him only at the request of the archpriest. After he received his blessing, he returned to his closed circle, glad to have gotten rid of all those useless formalities.

48

But the current Vladika was different from all his predecessors. This was undeniable. Even Father Gherasim noticed his originality, but... if the heavens did not answer his sighs, what could an archbishop do?

Only one thing interested Father Gherasim now – the fate of his friend, Father Paul. His case seemed to be a little out of the usual, so he wanted to see what could the attitude of the new Archbishop be towards it.

Therefore, Father Gherasim decided to wait for his colleague from the seminary.

IV

he first chimes wafted early over the barely awakened town, after which they were joyfully taken over by the rest of the bells, blending into a terrifying and powerful wave carried by the fresh wind of the morning. The echo covered the outskirts of the town and reached until the faraway surroundings.

The faithful from all over the place were heading towards the churches. Majority of them gathered at the monastery where, this time, the Archbishop was going to minister.

Father Paul had to walk a great distance until he would reach the monastery. When he entered the church, the priests were already ministering, and the believers were impatiently waiting for the Great Entrance.

Squeezing through the crowd, Father Paul managed to get in the front row and was now standing before the Royal Doors, from where he could see the new Archbishop better and also what was happening in the altar. He fixed his look on the Holy Table. In front of it, surrounded

49

by a group of priests in the middle of a cloud of incense, the Archbishop was praying.

Father Paul was mostly amazed by the absence of the fussing that usually characterized the Episcopal sermons. A godly silence was reigning on the altar. The majestic figure of the new Archbishop seemed to have frozen in the intensity of praying. The priests were standing quietly, stiffly and solemnly, in profound absorption. Their lips were whispering prayers and their eyes were set on the Holy Table. A long waiting had filled their gaze. It seemed that the servants were waiting for Someone Unseen since all of them thought that His coming depended on the intensity of their prayers. The more earnestly they would call Him, the more they would feel His presence amongst them and on the Holy Table.

But if their prayers and the strength of their spiritual grace subtly directed towards the heavens to the unseen God would weaken, then the reversed flow of Christ's Grace would break, leaving them without an answer from Him. They would leave the Holy Table disappointed and ashamed, incapable of boldly and joyfully looking in the eyes of the crowd that gathered at the monastery hoping to receive the Divine Grace; the people would feel deceived by the priests' spiritual weaknesses, for they are the mediators between Heaven and Earth.

Father Paul felt contained with a holy shivering. He unwittingly remembered stories of pilgrims who returned from Palestine and spoke of the Holy Fire, of how it descended at the Tomb of our Lord on the Great Saturday. He clearly saw the moment happening right now:

The crowd, composed of thousands of believers from different nations of the world, had gathered in the church. They are all in constant strain, waiting for the mystical moment to happen. All eyes are fixed on the Patriarch. Time is slowly passing. The solemn moment approaches. The crowd either frets noisily or freezes in astonishment. The Patriarch is aware of the enormous responsibility he carries and heads to the Tomb. He kneels in front of the marble stone, on the very spot where the body of Our Lord Jesus Christ had been buried. Fervently praying, he asks Him to send His Holy Fire. The waiting is painful – one minute passes. Then two, three. The Fire has not yet descended. A rumble can be heard in the church. At first, it is barely noticeable, but then it gets louder and rises higher until it finally collapses like an angry wave, reaching the ears of the Patriarch himself. The hierarch knows very well what the roar means. It's the crowd murmuring, disappointed by the weakness of his prayers. If he will not be successful in descending The Fire, the crowd will rip him apart. He gathers his last strengths and kneels down on the floor, plunging into prayer. Cold drops of sweat had covered his forehead. Suddenly, a tiny spark appears above the Tomb. Then another one. Then many others. Filled with happiness, the hierarch gets up and hurries to lit a bunch of candles from the sparks and solemnly brings them outside, sharing The Fire with the crowd. The people are on the verge of excitement. They grab the fire and kiss it. They kiss the Patriarch's hands and vestment while he, exhausted and powerless, with his duty fulfilled, rushes to leave the church.

Father Paul's analogy was not randomly made. Like the Patriarch of Jerusalem, Vladika was in a tormented spiritual waiting. With the same kneading, he was waiting for the prefiguration of the Holy Gifts, asking God to descend His Holy Spirit upon them. The Archbishop's voice betrayed his tension when he was emphasizing the words of the prayer he had to say according to the Typikon[11].

Father Paul felt confused when he heard the voice of the new Archbishop. It was strange, but it sounded familiar. He tried to remember where he had heard it before, but in vain. He was impatiently waiting for the Archbishop to turn his face towards the believers.

The moment of prefiguring the Holy Gifts ended. "Amen! Amen! Amen!" – the cheerful voice of the archdeacon was heard, and all the servants, with an endless gratitude towards the Lord, kneeled in front of His Holy Table.

Father Paul knew that, according to the Typikon, some singing would follow next, after which the Archbishop would turn around and bless the gathering. He stepped forward, so anxious to see the hierarch as better as he could that, without noticing, he pushed with his hand a lady's hat that was preventing him to see the Royal Doors. The lady turned and mumbled something angrily, but the Father ignored her.

At that same moment, the Archbishop appeared between the doors, facing the believers. Father Paul quickly fixed his eyes at him and froze on the spot. In front of him, dressed in episcopal

52

---

11 Typikon – A book of directives and rubrics that establishes the order of divine services for each day of the year in the Orthodox Christian Church. It assumes the existence of liturgical books that contain the fixed and variable parts of these services. In monastic usage, the Typikon of the monastery includes both the rule of life of the community and the rule of prayer.

vestments, with the miter on his head, stood the *priest* from the ship.

Father Paul's thoughts tangled together in his mind. He felt how something ignited inside him, then rotated, then stormily spun until it broke out, turning his face purple and red hot with embarrassment. Instinctively, he stepped back, trying to disappear into the crowd, away from the Archbishop's tracks. Vladika, however, did not seem to notice anybody. After throwing a glance at the crowd, he lifted his eyes towards the sky, blessed the people and returned to the altar.

"God, what have I done! What have I done?!" Father Paul was moaning, almost perceptible. "Whom have I dared to tempt with vodka?"

Somehow, he managed to listen to the sermon until the end and, without waiting for the people to scatter, he stormed towards the exit with the intention of leaving the town immediately.

"Father, hey, Father!" a voice from behind his back made him stop. He turned around and saw a Reader[12] who was trying to catch up with him. "Vladika asked me to inform you that, by all means, he'll be expecting you next Sunday evening..."

"I'm done for," thought Father Paul. "He saw me."

The crowd leaving the church squeezed and pushed the Father, dragging him outside the walls of the monastery.

Vladika remained to inspect the monastery. The abbey was especially renowned for its

---

12 Reader – Also called a lector, the Reader is the second-highest of the minor orders of the Orthodox Church. It is a clerical order to which a man is tonsured and ordained, setting him apart as blessed by the archbishop to read in services and in the Divine Liturgy.

wonder-worker icon to which rows of pilgrims, from almost every corner of Russia, would come and pray. The icon, which was beset with ornaments worth a few hundreds of thousands of rubles, had been placed in a golden shrine, in the most honorably spot of the monastery. It became its main relic and, as a matter of fact, the only glory of the huge monastic settlement.

The icon had been stolen not long before the arrival of the new Archbishop. All the believers were dismayed; never before had such blasphemy and profanity occurred in the entire country. The searching was in vain. The icon was thought to have disappeared from the monastery forever. A flood of accusation fell upon the monks stating they did not know how to preserve their treasure. Partially, they were just. The monastery was surrounded by an imposing wall over which no thief could climb. Still, in one place, the garden of the monastery was neighboring private property where, instead of a wall, there was a small wooden fence. Probably, nobody would have expected any danger to come from that particular entrance. But the thieves sneaked in and then sneaked out with the icon precisely through that spot. As it is very well known, a Russian's mind comes to its senses only after the event had happened. Thus, only after the icon had been stolen did the monastic brotherhood think of securing that area with a stone wall.

The idea had been vigorously put into practice. Now, instead of the old wood fence, there was a huge stone wall over which even a raven would be afraid of flying. The abbot was rightly proud of the new construction. He invited the Archbishop to see the structure, hoping that the new hierarch would recognize the efforts at their true value. However, he was disappointed. Vladika looked at it attentively and asked what was the price paid for building it. He shook his head and, turning towards his attendant monks, suddenly said:

"So, you have built a wall and believe that it will protect you from thieves now? You cannot fool thieves, but rather, you'll get exhausted. This method might have worked in the past when thieves would only rob at night, in the woods, when rogues and highwaymen could be recognized just by their clothes. Nowadays it's different. You all know there are so many thieves nowadays that there aren't enough prisons to contain them. Do you want them to stop threatening you? Then do not keep treasures which they seek! If you had left the wonder-worker icon the way that God Himself had left it, then there would have been little chance for the thieves to steal it. You have decorated it with gold and jewels... who do you think needs all this? Well, whoever did need it came and took it. Should I remind you, I wonder, that the human hands serve The Lord not because He would be in need of something? Some people show their gratitude and their faithfulness to God like that, for they can only serve Him with their wealth. And they gladly bring it to the monastery. Blessed be their gift! But *I desire mercifulness and not sacrifice*. Is it not you who are entrusted with the sacred duty of cleansing the sacrifices brought by people? Not every penny given to the monastery comes from righteous sources: some smell like sin and some even like blood. Therefore, purify all the silver and gold that you receive; melt and pass it through the furnace of your devotion. Everything that is given to the monastery must serve only as a shrine to the Light preached by the Gospel; the Light that cannot be hidden under a bushel basket. And even if you would decorate with gold the inner and outer walls of the house that shelter this Light, it will still not shine brighter. The Light will glow brighter only when you pour more oil, more myrrh, on it. You must transform all the money and all the things that come to the monastery in oil and myrrh. You understand what kind of myrrh I am talking about, don't you? The more of this myrrh you pour, the brighter the Light will shine. *Let your Light shine before men, so that they may see...* How do you continue this?"

Vladika quickly addressed the question to a monk who, from what he noticed, suffered from obesity. Not expecting such a blunt question, the monk lost his head and could not continue the evangelical text.

Vladika smiled and turned around, continuing to examine the area. He wanted to see the monastery grottoes, dug under it by its early founders. He discovered, in fact, an entire underground settlement. The dark chambers communicated with each other through bent and winding corridors spread all over the place. The corridors formed a labyrinth so convoluted that, without a guide, nobody would ever find the exit. The first ascetics came here. They used to spend their days and nights praying and constrained their intemperance of vices by digging new cells and corridors.

Nowadays, nobody lived in the caves anymore. They became a curious tourist attraction. The chambers were used to host old icons from the monastery. Tin canes and plates were carefully placed in front of them for the pilgrims who wanted to donate money. The visitors would feel frightened even from the entrance of the caves while the ladies would often faint. The ones who had visited the caves before confirmed having the feeling of being buried alive. Despite the presence of the guides and the many pilgrims armed with torches, the atmosphere would still be grim. What did the founders of these caves feel when they were working here in solitude, by the light of the oil lamp?

Vladika was pacing in a deep silence and, at one of the turnings, he stopped and asked:

"How old are these caves?"

"More than a hundred years old, Your Holiness."

"And in one hundred years"—asked Vladika thoughtfully— "no monk has ever considered following the example of these founding fathers, and dig at least one more foot?"

Approaching the exit of the cave, Vladika fixed his eyes on some heavy iron rings that had been hanging on the walls since the time of the first ascetics. They were massive, weighing at least one pood[13] each, and could be locked with a padlock.

"Behold, with such padlocks should you protect yourselves from thieves and within such

---

13 Pood – A Russian unit of mass equal to 36.11 pounds. Pood was first mentioned in a number of 12th-century documents.

walls should you find refuge," Vladika said, pointing to the iron rings then to the caves.

"What can we…" dared a monk to ask naively.

"Then why are you here?!" Vladika immediately interrupted him, fixing his eyes on all those present.

The monks kept silent. Also in silence, Vladika bowed to them and, without saying anything else, he left the monastery.

V

t was almost noon when the summer heat forced the townspeople to find refuge in cooling places, anywhere they could find any. Towards midday, a storm cloud rose in the sky from the south. The lightning flashed and the thunder immediately followed. A warm summer rain began to pour heavily, cleaning the dusty streets and houses. The town had been dressed in festive colors. Late in the afternoon, the wind dissipated the clouds, and the sun warmly shined into the west, gently caressing the azure sky and refreshing the boundlessness of the earth.

The townspeople had been lured out of their suffocating rooms and into the open air. Near the church of The Ascension of the Lord, a small circle of friends had gathered in a little garden surrounding the parsonage for a late afternoon tea.

The majority was comprised of students from average learning institutions. Among them was a passionate young man, a student at the Theological Academy and a relative of the parish priest, Serghei Dmitrievici Aliosin. Vladimir and Zosima, two priests and guests of the master of the house, were walking along the short alley of the garden. There was a big table situated in a discreet corner of the garden, covered with a white tablecloth. Here, the priestess was busy preparing tea in a huge samovar for the guests. The host himself, Father Grigori, was sitting at the other end of the table. On the sides of the table, the chairs were occupied by his old friends: the doctor – friend of the family – and Sadulla Mirzebekovici Addurahmanov, a merchant of Tartar origin and Father Grigori's neighbor.

The guests were invited to the table and, shortly, the tea was served. Father Zosima and Father Vladimir joined their confrere's company, while the youngsters formed a circle at the other end of the table. Soon after, the conversation started. Initially, about the weather, followed by recent events in which the Archbishop was briefly mentioned.

"Well, Father Grigori, what do you think about our new shepherd?" Father Vladimir addressed the host.

"Why would you ask him?" intervened the doctor. "Surely he will praise the new Archbishop. If we are to judge by what we've heard, he is the embodiment of Father Grigori's ideal. If you still remember"—he turned to Father Grigori— "you told me about his first speech to the clergy. He's got ideas identical to the ones you talk about in your preaching."

"It is true. I am delighted with our new Archbishop. I can tell from his actions that he is a sincere man who strongly believes in the Gospel and, in any case, is not a bureaucrat. There's something apostolic in him. Should there be more archbishops like him, we would probably not be living today in this decline of religiosity within the Russian society. I think the new Vladika can lead the clergy to the top again, including the religious spirit of our society. He will bring back the intelligentsia that separated from the church a long time ago."

"Well, listen to what you're saying... I cannot understand you Father, not by a long shot. According to the opinion that you've shared with us here, the intelligentsia separated from the church because of the priests. I even recall how, in one of your preachings, you mentioned that the intellectuals hate the church because the clerical guild only pursues its own narrow interests, not the ideals left by God. Do not insist, Father Grigori! Do you really think that the intelligentsia cannot distinguish between what is primordial and what is random, regarding the Church? Between the authentic Church— of insatiable priests and the teaching of Christ— and the preaching of some poor little priests filled with the theology of their own making? For instance, I am sure the intelligentsia did not abandon literature just because a variety of dubious scribblers have spawn lately. No! The reason must be searched deeper. The age when mankind would rely only on faith has passed. The age of reason now stands on its right. Mankind bit from the tree of knowledge and won't go back. For him, the data gained from science is more valuable than belief. Science has not had its final word yet. And if today we hear people speaking of its failure, then those

61

men are weak minded, unable to undertake the assiduous quest for knowledge. Either way, even the little pieces of information obtained through science are more precious to him than this foggy immensity of metaphysical or theological treasures. Science and faith, religion and reason continue to remain irreconcilable despite all the efforts to reconcile them. And the future belongs to science, of course, not faith; for as the saying goes: never quit certainty for hope. Thus, the true intellectuals who are veritable scientists will never be lured in the Church by neither your new Archbishop nor John Chrysostom himself!" the doctor submitted.

"I cannot agree with you on this, doctor. You are defending intelligentsia by saying that it can distinguish the accidental from primordial, but you have committed, in fact, the same error. You are saying that religion has died. Not true! Only some form or another of worshiping God may disappear. Religion has, is and will exist. Always! In the specific case of Christianity, we cannot say that it has been totally consumed. Christianity means preaching the Kingdom of Heaven and mankind has not come, not even close, to comprehend the entire expansion and profoundness of this Kingdom. The righteousness of Christ and the depth of His Kingdom are boundless. No epoch can lay claim of having fully discovered Christ's righteousness..."

"Then you should first discover *all this righteousness of Christ* if you consider that neither Christ himself nor His Apostles have discovered it and present it to the world. Perhaps then, mankind will understand something of it, or better yet, accept it. But for the moment, of all that has been discovered or well, disclosed, nothing can be digested by the human mind yet. Only the Christian morality can be understood..."

"Please, if you allow me," Father Vladimir intervened. "You are claiming that nowadays reason cannot accept Christian truths in all their fullness. This doesn't mean that it will never accept or understand them in the future. Reason progresses, knowledge expands, science is enriching with new experiences... But for now, there is nothing left to do than to believe. To have faith. Go to church, light some candles, do prostrations and look for hope to the priest. Will he relieve you of your sins or not? Will he unlock for you the doors of the Kingdom to the Other World or not?"

"Well now, we have again mixed the accidental with the fundamental," noticed Father Grigori.

"It is imperative to distinguish between the essence of Christianity and its ritual aspect!"

"Well, can you imagine that I have not yet been able to find an answer to the question: what is the actual essence of Christianity in general and of Orthodoxy in particular?"

"Behold the person who I believe can answer your question," said the mistress of the house, waving her hand towards the gate entrance.

At that moment, Pavel Ivanovici Iulanov entered the courtyard. He could easily be recognized by the solemn appearance and the well-tempered walking. Pavel Ivanovici, a professor at the Theological Academy, was known in the academic world for his massive paper works on Christian exegesis. In his free time, he used to pass by Father Grigori's house for a chat.

"Pavel Ivanovici! Hello and welcome. You are just in time," said Father Grigori.

"Good day, beloved Fathers," Pavel Ivanovici greeted everybody, maintaining his solemn attitude and outstretching his white and chubby hand to those present.

"Well, as you can see, our conversation has just spanned into your area of expertise," said the doctor. "We were arguing about why did the intelligentsia separate from the Church, from religion. Father Grigori places the entire blame on the priesthood. If we are to accept his opinion, then it would be sufficient for priests to start preaching sincerely and passionately and to minister God's sermons with more zeal. Then everything should be wonderful. Then all of these Kit Kitîci would give all of their riches to the poor, ministers would embrace the lackeys, students would light candles in front of the icons, and the prima donnas of the theatres would teach and bless their fans, before sleeping with them, to devoutly love only their legitimate wives! No matter what you say, Father Grigori, honesty alone is not enough. Remember the fate of my younger brother? He was honest, disinterested and kind in such a way that he would share even his last crust with his neighbor? He started drinking for reasons I do not know. It could be that heredity had its way. He kept drinking and drinking. Did I not urge him to abandon this vice? And were not my words sincere? I talked and wrote to him. I wrote to him with the blood of my chest, as one of your bishops used to say, asking the priests to do the same in their preaching! Admittedly, the words worked. The poor man stopped drinking. But one week later he hanged himself. There you have it; the sincerity of preaching."

"Too narrowly did you understand me, doctor," replied Father Grigori. "I did not speak only of preaching and teaching, but also of the many good things that Christianity can offer to the world."

"Then, would you be so kind and explain to me what these good things are, these principal things that Christianity had offered to mankind so far?"

"Christianity deserves a lot of merits, doctor," Father Vladimir intervened again. "Allow me to mention a few. First of all, Christianity changed the notion of family, by changing the status of women; from slaves to helpers to their husbands. It offered them human dignity and equal status to man. Secondly, children have been entitled to equal treatment from other people. You know, of course, that in the past parents had the right to sell their own children as slaves. Then Christianity radically changed the relationships between masters and slaves, initially tempering and, later on, completely abolishing slavery and serfdom. It improved the attitude towards work, absolving it from the stigma of shame. It gave birth to social life, by placing the commandment of loving God and the neighbor, which actually means love all mankind, in the forefront. It relaxed legislation and ennobled humans in general. The influence of Christianity can mostly be observed in the changes made to individual ethics. A new type of man has been created."

"There is the Christian man who has Christian feelings, a Christian will and a Christian disposition."

"Wonderful!" the doctor didn't give up. "But Christianity did all this in the past. These merits form, let's say, its historical merits. Today, parents who sell their children can only be seen at the menagerie. Nowadays cannibals are the only ones who need Christianity, for they don't know that their neighbor is meant to be served and not roasted on a spit. This also applies to Turks; to attribute women equal status to men. However, as far as the intelligentsia is concerned, only a naïve seminarist can still try to teach about its morals lessons, now that all these rules have been written down in the books used by children to learn how to read. By the way, if you have noticed, the majority of the complaints in the media nowadays refer to priests preaching less and less while preaching, as a type of activity, is disappearing. The priesthood is silent. Why? Has laziness overwhelmed them? This is only a tiny part of the truth. Take a better look at them—only the most intelligent and serious are silent while blabbers, like your parish neighbor, prefer to continuously fire away preachings at Liturgies, at Vespers, at Matins and during their entire free time. As a result, even those who used to come to church have stopped coming. The truth is that priests have realized they don't have anything new to say to people. Thank God, the intelligentsia is educated. It can read the Gospel by itself and can find the necessary explanatory notes when needed. And it can do it just as well as any of you. Both ethics and theology are accessible, and if someone would need help, they could easily ask a teacher, a master, or a professor."

"I must agree with you on this," said Father Grigori. "Moral ideals and life lessons can indeed be found in books. But isn't this precisely the reason why all these rules remain only in the written word? Isn't it for this that the world today has become so narrow, so suffocating that everything remained just simple words and life has taken a totally different path? Speaking about lively preaching, I wanted to point out that only by example, only by implementing the Christian teaching into our lives, our actions, and decisions, can we obtain the liveliness of Christ's righteousness."

"So, according to what you said, priests must not only teach but also live what they preach? Wonderful! I have to say that neither in this case should we set our hopes high. Allow me a riddle: why did Konovalov hang himself? Couldn't he find a man worthy of carrying on his disinterested ideals? But alas, the same Konovalov, under a different name, from a story called The Orlovs by the same author, enters a hovel full of cholera patients and meets some doctors. Here, doctors represented the embodiment of selfless servicing to their neighbor. Why then, while his wife found the meaning of her life here, did Orlov abandon her and his ideal and went into the wild world, repaying good with evil?

"In fact, why only give literary examples? Let's take a real-life one. You know, of course, Father Gherasim, the one looking after the people at the asylum. Could we ever find a more selfless man than him? He has totally committed himself to serving his neighbor. He went all the way with his serving; he preaches, he cures, he buries, and he nearly delivers babies. He is a living example of a dedicated pastoral mission. And what is the result? Who followed him? I've seen how he treats his patients. He caresses and convinces them to quit drinking. They stop drinking for one year or two, after which they re-start it more vigorously. Despite his superhuman struggles, none of the vagabonds turned out to decent yet. Indeed, they do love him, but in their own way; they appreciate him, kiss his hands, his feet, but, in the end, they snatch his last pennies and get drunk. What has the Father received in exchange of his virtuous service? He has ruined his life. What do you have to say about this, professor?!"

All the eyes were fixed on Iulanov. Long moments of silence have passed. The youth, who was eavesdropping for quite some time, had quieted down permanently. The student, Serghei Dmitrievici, set his gaze on Pavel Ivanovici. The professor leisurely drank up his glass then began to speak in a tone suited for a classroom:

"Gentlemen, in your reasoning, you've lost sight of some essential aspects, which is why your subsequent conclusions risk of becoming heretical. If you concentrate too much on the doctrine, you stray towards Protestantism. And if you prioritize ethics in excess, you have all the chances to adhere to Tolstoyism. And if..."

"Here's a thing I cannot accept!" a harsh voice came from the middle of the youth. The student, Serghei Dmitrievici, stood up without concealing his irritation and, abandoning all good manners, assaulted the appalled professor:

"What is it with this despicable habit, this mischievous practice of labeling every word: *this is Protestantism, this is Tolstoyism, this is heresy...?!* You have divided all the human ideas into categories and, despite that, you are at peace with yourself! People struggle and suffer in their attempt to understand the essence of religion, of Christianity, of Orthodoxy for God's sake! And you are calmly naming '*this is Protestantism, this is Molocanism[14]...*' Please, tell us clearly and in simple words: What is, in fact, the essence of Christianity?!"

"Young man," replied the professor, feeling offended. "You should not have forgotten the textbooks from the seminary. But if you have, I dare to remind you of the basic doctrines of Christianity regarding the Divine Trinity, about the incarnation of the Son, about His Resurrection from the dead, His Redemption of mankind..."

"And so on and so forth..."— the student interrupted— "See the contents of Macarius's book on dogmatics, etc... Please understand us correctly, Pavel Ivanovici. Our discussion is not about the fundamental dogmas of Christianity and their importance, but about what Christianity hides in itself; that something essential and seductive, which would act as unstoppable on people and would persuade them to become, first of all, religious, then convert them to Christianity and not to Islam or Tolstoyism, etc." Tolstoyism, etc."

"Everything is good in Christianity, Serghei Dmitrievici," Father Grigori interrupted him.

69

14 Molocanism – Sect in the Tsardom of Russia.

"Show me one single thing that is, undoubtedly, evil..."

"It's not about good or evil. Everything may be good, but to what use if all these things are, in fact, a deception? Who needs varnish even if shines? People don't abandon Christianity because it feels cheap to them, or they've found another superior religion to practice. The reason is that they are disappointed by its truthfulness. In this case, we cannot do anything with our ontological reasoning or any other reasoning for that matter; they are not convincing enough. The more such arguments are gathered, the more people run away from religion and the Church. It is the time we give the matter a thought. It's not a theology crisis. It's a crisis in the very heart of Christianity. As long as you cannot prove its authenticity or inalterability, you will not convince anyone to receive it. Its rightfulness is not clear enough for everybody. Let's use an example. Let's assume you are a wine dealer. A customer wants to buy some wine. You pour the wine into a bottle, praising it. You tell the customer that your wine is the best wine, the only natural one, which cannot be found anywhere else. It is produced by a brilliant winemaker who is a complete unusual man and, what is more, he's not the only one. He owns the winery together with three other men. The customer buys the wine, however, not because you praised it so cleverly, but because he needs it. The wine gives him pleasure so he finds it useful. He tasted it and found it to be good.

"On the contrary, if the wine is sour or acidic, no matter how hard you try to convince him of the opposite, he won't believe you. In fact,

70

not only will he not buy it, but he will suspect you of bad intention and that you have tried to persuade him into buying an expired product on purpose. This is what has happened with theology and the representatives of the Church: soon enough, people will openly call priests, including yourselves Fathers, to be liars and scoundrels, precisely because of your zeal to protect Orthodoxy..."

"It looks like we have strained away from the subject of our discussion," noticed Father Vladimir. "We were talking about the essence of Christianity. It has become very clear to us now what this essence is about. This essence can precisely be compiled by the Christianity's moral part, Serghei Dmitrievici. The uplifting evangelical love and the holy righteousness of Christ are fascinating. The goodness itself is priceless. Its usefulness doesn't need to be proved."

71

"I fully agree with you, Father Vladimir," said Father Grigori. "And there is nothing left for us to do than to teach everyone this value, this evangelical pearl so that mankind will accept it without any validation!"

"So now we are back to square one," smiled ironically the doctor. "Please, do not forget my initial remarks: Firstly, the goodness is not fascinating for everybody. For Kit Kitîci, a bag filled with gold is far more fascinating. You are fascinated by the beautifulness of moral ideals, while I— by the thick, naked legs of a lady dancer. And secondly, the goodness is helpless. I may have reached the conclusion that happiness is a virtue, but that doesn't mean at all that I'll become a virtuous person. I would like to be one but I can't. Apostle Paul says: 'I do not do the good I want, but I do the evil I do not want.' It is a universal tragedy, with millions of victims, including my poor brother. He understood both the misery of his horrible vice and the benefits of a virtuous renewal. He wanted to quit but couldn't. And for attempting to fight his vice, he paid the ultimate price: his life. This is the true subject of our dispute. And there are no contradictions. You are researchers and speak about the fundamental value of Christianity. I acknowledge this value, however, I grant it the status it deserves."

"And what would this be, if you do not mind our curiosity?"

"And what would this status be, if you do not mind our curiosity?"

"The status of books about good manners, in a society that respects itself!"

"It is impossible to have a conversation with you, doctor! You only speak in paradoxes..."

"Come on, seriously now! What has religion offered to man? What is the meaning of this multitude of rites and sermons that our Christian Orthodoxy, in particular, consists of? For instance, we celebrated the patron saint of our church last week. The priest went from house to house, sprinkling holy water. He came to my house too. He overzealously sprinkled it; he wet the papers on the desk, then my walls, ruining my precious photographs. My wife is still upset because of the velvet upholstery furniture. So tell me now, what is the use of all this sprinkling of water?"

"This custom existed since the Old Testament," answered timidly Father Zosima. "It is the symbol of our cleansing!"

"Well see, this is exactly why I am asking about the meaning of all these symbolic acts. If this is an illustrative method of explaining the Christian truths, then, like I said before, the intelligentsia is in no need of such teachings anymore. Perhaps someone still needs an icon to channel his thoughts towards the Figure represented on it. As for me, such a reminder is absolutely useless. I do not suffer from memory loss. I can still remember God wherever I want: in the train station, in the carriage, at the theatre. In my point of view, all these things are pointless."

"You see! You see!" interrupted the professor triumphantly. "I told you that you would deviate to Protestantism! You have brilliantly demonstrated just that! And the rest of you, gentlemen, have made a mistake when indicating the actual essence of Christianity. The essence of Christianity lies not in its moral aspects, but in its dogmatics. The Christian morals were known in the ancient world too. For a complete discovery, it wasn't necessary for The Son of God to be sent to Earth. It would have been enough if a prophet like Moses would have written a new Tablet of the Law. The ones who turned their attention exclusively to Christian ethics did it not in vain, if you allow me this parenthesis, for they eventually denied the divine nature of its founder and reduced Him to the dignity of a great ethic reformer. However, if we take the dogma of Redemption of mankind by the Son of God as the starting point in our argumentation and use the

73

path of the most severe logical operations, then we can justify some liturgical particularities such as the sprinkling of holy water."

The professor took a break, casting a satisfied glance to all those present. The silence was broken by a dull sound, which resembled a sigh or a moan, coming from the chest of Serghei Dmitrievici.

"Enough with the logic already!" he started. "Even the middle-school first-year students started to blame the seminarists from scholastics. We want life! We see in front of us the exact life that our contemporaries live and challenge Christianity... Redemption... Salvation... Resurrection... Revival... Transformation... The Old Man... The New Man... The Power of God... Grace... These terms have set our teeth on edge ever since the seminary. Have teachers failed to understand that all these are but words, words, and words? Words that don't have any meaning or lost it a long time ago? For almost two thousand years has the whole world been hearing of these words but not even today has it been able to understand what kind of Resurrection, Revival, Transformation had really happened. The world had a religion before Christ and another one after Him. The life of the people didn't suffer much, except for some doctrinal changes in thought, feelings, and attitudes. In its essence, mankind remained the same. The only thing that had taken place is what Father Vladimir mentioned about the Christian merits.

"However, in the life of one particular man, something did happen that L.N. Tolstoy brilliantly described in his novel, Resurrection. The main character, Knez Nehliudov, is living like

74

a scoundrel, causing terrible things to people. Then he understood how filthy his actions were and changed his opinions. He stopped to behave degradingly and began to lead a normal life. That is the whole Revival, the whole sense of Resurrection!"

"You are making a big mistake, young man. Christianity does not take at all into account this type of resurrection," the Professor said, giving the student a very severe look.

"Then what type?! Tell me!" the student was almost shouting. "I understand the Church's teaching about Christ's Resurrection. Christ has resurrected, of course, but not in this sense. He literally died and rose from the dead. All we can do is either believe it or deny it. But since Christ's Resurrection, no other man had risen from the dead! They used to die before Christ and still die after Him. This is not my objection; it had been brought upon the first Christian preachers. Read Apostle Peter's epistle. The Apostles were preaching to the world about the triumph over death, about the Resurrection. But, in their own experience, people noticed that the power of death did not diminish at all, for their eyes would still see dead people every day. The Apostles discharged this contradiction, emphasizing the ancient teachings of the resurrection of the dead. Probably, only the Sadducees and the Epicureans were the only ones that did not believe it. As an argument in favor of resurrecting from the dead, the Apostles would bring forward a singular case of resurrection; Christ's Resurrection: 'If Christ has not been raised, then our preaching is in vain.' Certainly, this reference was convincing at that time. But now, when Christ's Resurrection itself is questioned, you will not attract intelligentsia to the church with all the teachings about resurrection and the afterlife because, in its opinion, the Kingdom of God has as many possibilities of existence as Mohammed's heaven has."

"Christ's Resurrection has been established as undeniable!"

"How? By proving the authenticity of the Gospel? How can you be sure that tomorrow, the newspapers won't publish news of some random oriental archaeologist who discovered new pieces of the Gospel? There have been similar cases in the past! If that will be the case, then a Christian with a sincere belief will have to endure agonizing doubts until some apologist will invalidate the finding."

76

"Anything can be disproved. Our discussion doesn't have an ending..."

"This is not true, not for a man with common sense at least. A straight line is the shortest path between two dots – only the opaque mind of a geometer needs proof for this. In life, this fact is universally accepted and any hurried carter would certainly take that road. Undoubtedly. If you present such axiom in dogmatism to mankind, it will accept it without the need for proof. The problem lies precisely here, in the Christian truths; no matter how moral they are, they cannot be justified in the passing life. This makes room for endless disputes. I apologize, but I must say it bluntly: you, Pavel Ivanovici, are a professor, a doctor of theology, a pillar of the Church and Orthodoxy in some way. You consider yourself a truly faithful Christian. You have been baptized, consecrated and wedded. You confessed and received the Holy Communion many times. Sadulla Mirzabekovici is a Mohammedan. What is the difference between you two? Show me one single evidence that helps us understand you have been cleansed and he has not, that you have been born over and he has not, that you have Christ within and you are indeed a new man, a new being in Christ, and he, well, he is a slave of the devil, an old man who will rot in his lusts. For example, I can distinguish between an intellectual and a boorish churl. But your case is totally different. In reality, I see two nicely dressed man, pretty much of the same, standing in front of me. You, Pavel Ivanovici, suffer from gout while Sadulla Mirzabekovici from asthma. He's got a wife and children. You have no children and your wife left you a long time ago. Both of you will die and your bodies will rot; you, with the hope of going into the Heavenly Jerusalem and he— into the wonderful heaven of Mohammed. But where you will actually land nobody knows!"

77

The student finished his words and fell on the chair. The guests, confused by his escapade, involuntarily kept silent. The priestess insisted on serving tea while Father Grigori addressed Father Zosima:

"And you Father, what do you think is the essence of Christianity?"

Father Zosima, a kind-hearted old priest, did not have theological studies but enjoyed listening to such debates even though he didn't take part in them. Father Grigori had asked him with the hidden purpose of ending this unpleasant discussion.

"What I think is this," started Father Zosima surprised. "In our priestly gramata[15] stands written: *Bring and give us, meaning to the archbishops, the greatest or most difficult things to judge.* So there, I think of asking our new Vladika about all this."

"Well, you've said it!" laughed the doctor. "Why do you need Vladika if we have such an important figure among us, like Pavel Ivanovici, a professor at the academy and doctor of theology? Vladika has only a doctorate degree and, between you and me, he had obtained it by the skin of his teeth, if we are to believe the information spread around by our curious little priests."

"Well, I don't know about that but, in my opinion, we should go to Vladika," insisted Father Zosima.

The doctor shrugged his shoulders. Father Vladimir smiled indulgently towards Father Zosima's blind confidence in the authority of the Archbishop while Father Grigori didn't say anything.

Pavel Ivanovici suddenly remembered an urgent matter and, after excusing himself, he hurried away.

The discussion was not going anywhere and, moreover, it was already late. The sun had set leaving the garden in the twilight. The guests exchanged a few more words and, after finishing their tea, they parted.

78

---

15 Gramata – A document, certificate, decree of blessing used specifically within the Church.

VI

wo days after the arrival of the new Archbishop, the town clergy had been informed by their archpriests that Vladika planned on visiting all the churches in town. Parish priests were told to be present and greet the Archbishop as a simple visitor, without any fuss and chimes.

The bustle of preparations began in each church. Everything was washed and cleaned. The ecclesiarches attentively examined every corner of the churches in search of any spider webs left unnoticed. They also checked if the floor had been polished well enough and if the candelabrum was shiny. The priests had thoroughly verified their churches' registers and tidied the Diaconicon and other objects in the Holy Altar. Everybody was trying to do their best. Nobody wanted to upset the new Archbishop, not from his very first days in the parish.

But at Father Gherasim's church, things were left untouched. After reading the notice from the archpriest, the Father hid it in a book and seemed to had completely forgotten about it. Erioma, who learned about Vladika's visit from a friend in town, recovered from his usual laziness and came running to Father Gherasim for the keys of the church. To his great surprise, the Father refused to give them and, in general, did not give him any other tasks.

"But Father, Vladika is going to visit all the churches... We should sweep, wash and carpet the floor, at least..."

"There's no need for that," answered curtly Father Gherasim.

The keeper left shrugging his shoulders.

"Why should I care?!" grumbled Erioma, heading towards his little shack. "You'll be the one getting burned anyway... My job is to obey... *Do as you're told...*"

In front of the church, there was a small lawn crossed by a wide pathway. Observing the litter pile that had been ruining the entire aspect of the church for quite some time, Erioma decided to sweep it away. He armed himself with a broom and a shovel and got busy. He gathered the litter and threw it on the pathway from where it was easier to load it in the trash bins.

Lacking support from Father Gherasim, Erioma's enthusiasm had soon weakened. His broom was heard more and more rarely and his shovel worked less and less convincingly. In the end, he stopped, slammed the tools to the ground and stuck his hand in his pocket to grab his mahorka[16].

80

---

16 Mahorka – Tobacco of low quality that poor people used to combine with thin paper or newspaper, forming their daily cigarettes. Creating such a cigarette takes time and requires attention to details.

He heard a strange noise, sounding partly like a song partly like a hum, coming from the open window of his chamber. It seemed that someone was crying, praying, moaning, singing, and laughing, all at the same time.

"Great guns, she's yelling again..." he grumbled angrily, throwing an upset look towards the window. "When did she manage to get drunk?"

He spat on the grass, plunged the shovel into the litter pile and left the church.

The strange sounds continued to be heard from behind the window. Erioma's wife, Pascuda, was howling. Her real name was Prascovia, but it had been more than five years since Erioma re-baptized his wife as Pascuda, so the rest of the world had picked it up too. Soon enough, Prascovia herself got used to the new name and accepted it as something natural.

There was a time when the current Erioma, the former Eremei Evstigneevici, would call his wife Pashenika and would overwhelm her with warm caresses. That time had irreversibly passed and had been long forgotten, sinking somewhere into the darkness. Life does not like to joke. Life is such a terrible mystery! The one who understands its meaning is rewarded with joyfulness while the one who light-mindedly hunts it will end up torn apart.

The young Eremei Evsigneevici, the master's favorite journeyman, and he, himself, soon-to-be a master, joyfully and carelessly stepped into the world together with his Pashnika, the daughter of a petty merchant. They had a big wedding with lots of dancing and partying, going on the loose ever since. But the drinking, the parties, and the ever-present guests had opened the doors to poverty as well. It's difficult to fight old habits. It's difficult to stop a rolling stone halfway the mountain.

Eremei Evsigneevici was the first to degrade and became the ever-drunken Erioma, losing his way. Shortly after, Prascoviushka followed in his footsteps. The sweet wines have been replaced with plum brandy, the snacks and lunches with coarse bread and rotten fish, the hot tenderness with ferocious beatings. Prascovia became Pascuda. The spouses would get drunk then fight, would fight then get drunk, hastily falling more and more into the abyss.

They came to the asylum. Here, they met Father Gherasim. The feeling of shame had been awakened in them, so the couple abandoned themselves in the hands of the priest. They moved into the keeper's small house, whose duties Erioma took over.

In the end, Erioma accepted his fate in his heart and was thankful and grateful to the Father, for the priest offered them a roof over their heads, including the possibility of working for food there. However, Erioma continued to drink his vodka in secrecy, giving up the fight with his nasty habit.

For Prascovia, the first weeks in the keeper's house had flashed hazily. Gradually, she found herself engrossed in the housework and stopped drinking all of a sudden. Her behavior suffered radical changes; cheerful in her youth, crazy in her drinking days, she had now transformed into a gloomy, grumpy and silent woman. Nobody could understand the interior, quiet conflict that Erioma's wife was living. Her husband would feel pity for her whenever he would see her sufferings. "She should drink rather than torturing herself like this," he would often think.

There were still some lucid moments in the life of the poor couple. Most often, they would happen before the holidays. After having locked the church, Erioma would give the key to Father Gherasim and would return home. Prascovia, who would arrive home several minutes before him, would prepare the samovar for tea. At first, they would quietly sip their tea, striving not to look at each other. Slowly, the conversation would fall into place, shaping into a peaceful and warm dialogue. They would try not to remember their previous life, but sometimes they would not resist; they would interrupt the conversation, immersing themselves in the gloomy memories of their former happiness. In some evenings, they would feel that their old life could be revived. In one of such evenings, while the samovar was hissing gently and the hot tea was warming and caressing their limbs, Erioma dared to talk about the happiness that could have been so possible. Prascovia sighed, desolately nodded her head and, looking somewhere on the horizon, she said:

"Had we had a child, maybe our life would have been different."

Erioma cast down his eyes in silence, realizing that his wife had just revealed her deepest desire. He too would often sigh, admitting that this was the affliction that had poisoned their life. But the situation was irreversible, so he had made peace with it.

83

Prascovia, on the contrary, did not. After their last talk, she began to behave oddly. She would suddenly start crying, grind her teeth and groan in convulsive roaring for no apparent reason. Things went from bad to worse. She had started drinking again and, at the same time, she began to howl. The 'tears of drunkenness' would transform into hysterical sobbing, and the sobbing would become hysterical waves of laughter, interrupted by calm monologues that would end in sad little melodies or heartbreaking howls. The tantrums would last an hour, sometimes two, after which Prascovia, frowning and depressed, would calm down and do her chores.

At first, Erioma tried to calm down his wife as much as he could, but she would always greet him with a torrent of the most selected curses learned at the asylum. So he gave up the idea and would hide somewhere far away during the crises. His most often hiding place was the tavern across the street. In search of comfort, he would double the quantity of alcohol he would usually drink and would fall asleep under the table. When he would wake up, he would try to straighten himself and would hurry to meet Father Gherasim. If the Father would happen to be in the courtyard, Erioma would grab the shovel with his shaky hands and would zealously start digging in places where, often times, there was no need. From time to time, he would throw inquisitive looks to Father Gherasim, stopping only when he would be sure that he would not lose his place there.

Erioma was certainly not the most suitable person to be a keeper, but neither did Father Gherasim prove to be the most exigent master.

84

Because of Father Gherasim's impassive attitude towards the ecclesiarch, Erioma would only wave his hand whenever the ecclesiarch would visit the church, after which he would return back to his business.

Initially, the news of Vladika visiting their church had mobilized Erioma. He had the sincere intention to clean up, but the indifference of the Father, and especially Pascuda's howling, broke his spirit. He plunged the shovel into the litter pile and abandoned his intention.

85

VII

 he day of the Archbishop's visits had arrived. Because he was detained by certain matters, Vladika left the eparchial courtyard only late at noon, roaming the streets of the town in his carriage.

The church inspections were performed in a rush. The carriage would quickly go from one church to another, spending no more than a few minutes for each.

The gossips, however, would arrive before the Archbishop's carriage. At the remaining churches, it had already been known what Vladika said in such or such place, what his opinion about the members of the parish council had been or what other things had been praised or disapproved by him. These gossips were taken seriously by Father Grigori too, the parish priest of the Holy Ascension Church, who was waiting in the altar for the vigorous visitor.

Father Grigori was of a dynamic, sentimental temper. For quite some time, he had been following the ongoing church life both in the eparchy as well as in the entire country. He noticed all the faults and had been suffering deeply. He would often pray in secrecy for God to send them a shepherd according to their heart.

The first impression he had after meeting the new Archbishop, plus the rumors that reached his ears, gave him hope that his prayers had finally been answered.

He traversed the altar several times, gazing through the window and feeling his heart pounding in a joyful waiting. He made the sign of the cross on himself from time to time, but he could not concentrate on his prayer. His heart was heavily pumping and, in his mind, a verse from the Scriptures, with no connection to the happenings, took the shape of different tunes and began playing: *'Pour rain upon the thirsty land, our Savior!'*

However, it was not meant for him to see Vladika that day.

The road from the Church of John the Baptist continued up, ending on a plateau where the largest part of the town could perfectly be seen. Vladika went up there and examined the panoramic landscape for a few moments. In the distance, he spotted a metal cross inclined on the top of a dome darkened ahead of its time. By knocking on the carriage window, he signaled the coachman to take him there.

This was the church of Father Gherasim.

In the past, the archbishops would not come here, so the Father had little hope of seeing the new Vladika at his church, but he still found it necessary to respect the indications given by the archpriest. Stepping impassively over the pile of garbage left behind by Erioma, the Father unlocked the church, remained on the doorstep, and waited, facing the road.

To his astonishment, he did not have to wait long. The carriage appeared at the end of the street. A few minutes later, it stopped in front of the church gate. The carriage door opened, revealing the Archbishop who had already started rushing towards the church. On the way, he was bewilderedly staring at the pile of trash that needed to be avoided and stopped at the entrance.

He was greeted by the dreary walls of the church. The daub, which had fallen off in patches, looked like an open wound, and the low arches, blackened ahead of their time, had been covered with a thick layer of dust. The dark, cobwebby corners darkened the expression of the Archbishop's face. Vladika took a few steps forward and stopped in front of the iconostasis. The sad, barely distinguishable faces of the saints were hopelessly staring at him.

Vladika made the sign of the cross on himself and stepped inside the altar. Father Gherasim stopped at the pulpit.

The altar was even less bright. The opaque window let little light come in, the Holy Table was dusty, and inside the Diaconicon, he could only find two or three worn vestments[17].

After inspecting the altar, Vladika went out to the pulpit and took one last look inside the

89

---

17 Two or three worn vestments – *(for Russians)* Represents carelessness towards the church rite. In the Russian Church, each holyday has its own liturgical color. These colors are: red for Pascha and for martyrs, blue for the Mother of God, green for pious men, white for Sunday, yellow for regular days, black and violet for The Great Fast and the holydays with strict fasting.

church before questioningly turning to Father Gherasim. The Father replied with a silent look.

A couple of minutes passed in silence.

Vladika kept looking at Father Gherasim— a worn out cassock patched in places, a crooked back, gray hair, a face still young but furrowed with deep cuts, dull eyes, a frail chest, long skinny arms. The Archbishop's eyes reflected a tormenting concern. Suddenly, he turned his face towards the altar, made a large cross sign on himself, prayed before the Holy Doors, and rushed to the door, leaving the church.

"Come!" he said, walking past Father Gherasim. The Father locked the church and followed the Archbishop.

When they reached the carriage, Vladika ordered the coachman to go home alone and unharness the horses, then addressed the Father:

"There are many things that I must talk with you... Let's go to your house."

"But, Your Grace," hesitated the Father, "That is not possible... I don't have a place."

"What do you mean you don't have a place? Where do you live then?"

"I mean, I have a house, but..."

Father Gherasim was completely intimidated. He stopped talking and cast his eyes down, while his face turned pallor. Suddenly, he straightened his back and firmly said, looking somehow enigmatically at Vladika:

"This way, Your Grace."

When someone is wounded, he rushes to the doctor, quickly showing him the wound, and suffers when the doctor touches it. The patient accepts to have his wound examined because he hopes that relief will follow after.

But things change when the whole body hurts, enduring an endless, unbearable and excruciating pain. In this scenario, the patient refuses to be examined because he is sure there is no cure left for him. He denies all help, writhes in agony and cries in a heartbreaking voice: "Let me be, for God's sake, leave me alone! Don't torture me! Let me die in peace!"

Experiencing the first wounds of his soul, the young and inexperienced Father Gherasim turned to his archpriest, searching for a healer. The experience was bitter but it had opened his eyes: he understood that he would never find a doctor and since then he had neither shown his wounds nor let anyone touch them.

The Archbishop's questioning looks in the church, the request to talk to him at his home, privately, made it clear to the Father that the state of his mind did not go unnoticed by his superior. A less perspicacious man could have scolded him at the sight of the deterioration in the church, and the Father was hoping precisely for that to happen– for him to be punished and then left alone. This would have allowed him to keep his *Holy of Holies* untouched. The new Vladika proved to be a bit more insightful, understanding that laziness and indifference were not the causes of the fall. In fact, it was the reflection of soul struggling which the parish priest was enduring, still unknown to the Archbishop. But the Archbishop decided to plunge deeper into the world that had opened to him at the entrance to the dreary church of Father Gherasim.

The Father felt it like an assault on his wounds. But the attacker had been a man who possessed all the power and who could not be refused. The Father thought of allowing his superior see his wounds so that afterward, shocked, the Archbishop will go away, letting him die in peace.

Vladika did not show any sign of amazement when he stepped over the threshold of Father Gherasim's house. It seemed that he was expecting to find it like that.

It was dark. Father Gherasim lit the lamp and offered his guest a chair.

The dim light of the lamp barely scattered the obscurity, projecting trembling, hardly distinguishable stripes of lights and shadows on the walls that were vanishing in the murky corners. The silence filled the room. The Father felt a nervous shiver taking over his body, and all his long-sufferings returned in his mind, giving birth to an endless flow of tormenting images of a former life. And now, while he was silently waiting for his superior's question, all these revived feelings were about to burst into a torrent targeted at the guest.

"The face is the reflection of the soul," Vladika began his words in a calm and gentle voice. "I have noticed in your eyes that neither laziness nor indifference is the real cause of the decay around. It is a more profound reason, still unknown to me. Actually, I can guess parts of it myself, but I 'd rather have you explain me. I have realized that it cannot be explained in just a few words, and for that reason, I have sent the carriage away. Do not rush. Use the time as you wish and, most importantly, ignore your superior's presence. Instead, remember that in front of you, is a bishop, a steward of the Holy Sacraments, the servant of God. And yours."

"I know"—the Father sharply intervened — "otherwise I wouldn't let you in." Then, everything that had been gathering over the years in the Father's soul burst out all at once...

He began his words clumsily, hastily, sometimes repeating himself, other times advancing too much. His nervousness prevented him from coherently expressing his thoughts. Yet, the more he dug in his memories, the more flowing, connected and opened his speech and story became.

He expressed the impacts of his childhood in vivid images, he serenely recalled his dreams from the seminary, he passionately spoke about his old ideas with which he stepped into life. But when he started talking about his first days as a priest, his voice began to tremble and remained like that for the rest of his story, despite his efforts of regaining his self-control. At one point, he seemed like he was about to reach the climax of a neurotic fever. His hands were shaking, his body was trembling, and his face was writhing spasmodically. His own helplessness would often interrupt the flow of the speech.

Vladika was listening strenuously, waiting in the chair with his hands covering his face.

When the Father spoke about the moment that had opened his eyes and revealed to him the *canker* of mankind, he jumped to his feet and began fussing around the room. The convulsions were chocking his voice, often interrupted by the hardly suppressed sobbing. Now, he

93

was impetuously talking about his spiritual dissensions, about the ordeals that followed, and about his doubt in the existence of God. It was hard, very hard to listen to him. It was the insanity of the demented speaking, the heavy howl of the blasphemer complaining.

The ending was cut off rather than concluded. With a deaf groan instead of a sigh, he exhaled the air kept all this time in his chest by the shortness of his breath and then stopped. Unexpectedly, he turned towards the Archbishop and fixed his piercing look on him. His eyes were filled with a sinister terror.

"Forgive us, Lord, and have mercy on us!" murmured shockingly Vladika. "Father Gherasim!... Calm down... Sit down... Listen to me!"

"Listen? What for?!" echoed the demented scream of the Father. "To prove me the existence of God, to comfort me with faith in the afterlife, to promise me the Heaven?... Oh, damned be those who can enjoy Heaven on behalf of the sighing and crying of the unfortunate sufferers on earth, on behalf of the mad gnashing of the sinners in hell! Let the ones who can delight themselves! I, for one, cannot! I do not wish such a Heaven..."

This was the final cry of a bleeding soul. The Father fell powerlessly on the chair and, by grabbing his head with both hands, burst out crying.

Vladika stood up and went to the corner where some icons were hanging and made the cross sign on himself several times. After that, he walked up and down the room with a profound concern. He stopped near Father Gherasim, made the sign of the cross on him three times, in silence, and hugged him.

A long time ago, in a distant past, lady Gherasim, his mother, whom he dearly loved, used to caress him like that. When he would return home for the holidays, young Gheraska would throw himself into her arms not resisting the joy of seeing his beloved mother. He would cry and tearfully tell her about all the hardships of a student's life. His mother would not say a word, but she would hold him tighter and tighter, smoothing his hair. The warmth of his mother's touch would quickly dry Gheraska's tears and, in no time, cheerful, alive and happy, he would run and would romp through the entire village. A long time had passed since then. Today, the Father caresses others, but his heart remained stone-cold, unjoyful, and the merciless life had slowly covered it with a veil of ice.

The caress from Vladika reminded him of his mother's. The long-forgotten sense of warmth had awakened in his chest and the ice began to melt.

The Father grabbed the Archbishop's hand and kissed it fervently several times.

"You see, much better now," said Vladika, understanding his hearted outbreak. "Now listen to me... You did not guess correctly. I will not comfort you with Heaven. I haven't been there and I don't know what's like there. And we shall not speak of things we personally don't know. Let us talk about what our eyes have seen, what they can see and what will they see."

Vladika had let his hands down, walked around the room again like he was gathering his thoughts, then leaned back in the chair and said:

"You have come to such a desperate state because you have seen other people's miseries. You have brought them upon yourself, and you have been horrified by the darkness of the pain that causes mankind to suffer. You have *discovered*, the *canker* of mankind, as you call it, but you have fallen into despair, conscious of your self-helplessness and your inability to do something."

"Yes, Vladika. Now you're going to explain to me that such things are only shallow tricks of a sick imagination... that the world won't cease to exist because of certain people's sufferings."

"Not at all. On the contrary, I want to say that you, who believe to have discovered this *canker*, have not uncovered even the hundredth part of it. What have you seen? A soaker from the asylum, eaten alive by syphilis, rotten and drowned in his own vomit? This has been the most illustrative example you've experienced in your life. The *canker* was in front of you; you've seen its rotting work, you've smelt its stench and understood how filthy, fetid, putrid and miserable man is. From the corpse of that drunkard, you've passed to other inmates, whose foreheads you noticed were marked with the same seal of the *canker*; mutilated noses, suspicious spots, ulcers...

"You've remembered how many asylums alike exist, how many taverns and brothels are dispersed across the whole world, and you calculated how many people are in all these places... And you have been terrified. Too soon.

Not only the dregs of society are eaten alive by syphilis; you would be surprised to find entire hamlets and villages infected with this disease, in almost all the countries in the world. Write them on your list. Then, carefully examine a *cleaner* society: will you not find the seal of the same *canker* here as well, under velvet and silk, under the snow-white lingerie?

"Now move on to the countless sanitariums, baths, and other curative establishments. There, patients coming from the high society make up for a good half of the clientele. Count them too. But it's not just syphilis that reaps people. Plague, leprosy, typhus, cholera, scab, tuberculosis... even a doctor would find it difficult counting all the existent diseases. The *canker* that is tormenting mankind has a thousand faces and, at the same time, they are all the same for everybody. The number of its victims equals the total number of people living on this planet. Its seal is marked on every human being. It lies on everyone, from the chubby face of a self-contented fat man to the pale acne-affected face of an anemic adolescent, or the lithe, thin face of a frail teenage girl. You can see it on the faces of men who fast; monks, priests, and laymen, kings and soldiers, parents and children. There isn't and never has been a man on earth who has not been affected by it. It's on everybody, including me and you..."

"What kind of *canker* can there be on you, Vladika?" asked Father Gherasim puzzled, glancing at the robust, imposing figure of the Archbishop, at his bright and beautiful face with sleek and rosy skin.

"This is precisely our struggle; we cannot see it. Our senses touched by the *canker* have become so blunted that we cannot perceive anything anymore. We cannot see the *canker* nor smell its reek. However, our blunt senses feel the *canker* only when a man lies on his deathbed and gives his last breath away. We can perceive it only when it grabs him, wraps him, eats him and permanently devours him, transforming him into what we call, a corpse. Then, we flee away from it, covering our noses from its terrible, horrible, cadaverous stench... Yes! Only then can we smell the miasma of death.

"The stench of the *canker* and the stench of death vary, for the *canker* itself varies. However, their essence is the same. Every man comes into this world carrying the *canker's* stench. Midwives know very well how the newborn babies and their mothers smell.

"The smell of this *canker* accompanies us our entire life... Can you not feel its smell on me? If not, then you cannot feel it on others either. Why? Because people succeed in covering the native smell of their body, more precisely of the *canker*, trough daily showers, through various baths and washing, through wiping, through freshening clothes with fresh air and sunshine and anointing them with different lovely-smelling ointments, through perfuming with the aroma of various cosmetic products. This is why we don't smell it.

"Yes, man smells awful... Take ten of the cleanest, healthiest people and lock them in a small chamber for a certain period of time. You'll notice how these clean people will taint the air with the smell of their breaths, with the emanations of their bodies. Keep them longer and you will see that they will begin to asphyxiate because of the stench and the musty, heavy, suffocating air. Think of a woman with a chaste, rosy-white, clean body. Take away all her perfumes. Prevent her from having a bath for three-four months, from changing her clothes, etc. You will notice the same heavy stench of the *canker*...

"Man lives in the atmosphere of the *canker*. He breathes it. His breath stinks with its reek. You know how people's mouths smell. You can distinguish the uncleanness by the food they ate. For some, this smell is so repulsive that it breaks the harmony of their marriage.

"The kingdom of the *canker* is enormous and man is not its only slave. Mankind is not the only creature that suffers, rots, decomposes and stinks horribly. Birds, animals, and insects are exposed to the same fate. *'For the entire creation groans together and travails together in pain, until now,'* says Apostle Paul. It's the result of the same *canker*. Its seal also marks the inanimate creation; the air sometimes reeks, the water goes bad, plants die and decompose while the decay prefigures the aroma of their flowers into the stench of rotten mold. It is the very morbid smell of the same *canker*. It is universal. It dwells on earth and in the ground. Its sap reaches the flowers from where the bees gather their honey. In this way, honey too can be poisonous to man..."

Vladika stood up, crossed the room a few times then sat down again. Father Gherasim was stiffly listening with maximum tension, following the thoughts of his interlocutor without ceasing to wonder at his—the larger, the more shocking— generalizations. And the deeper the Archbishop dived in his monologue, the greater Father Gherasim's astonishment grew. He did not expect such words coming from an archbishop. He would assume that Vladika, an intelligent but especially a thoughtful and sincere believer, would try to comfort him by exercising the usual messages, intertwined with verses from the Scripture— countless variations of the same topic on praying, patience, and devoutness. The Father had a reply prepared in case of such consolation, a reply based on real-life facts resulted from the upsetting contradictions of words and events amongst *people who use references to the Holy Scripture.*

Determined not to spare himself at all, the Father planned to throw even this poisonously and venomously reply to the Archbishop. To his great surprise, he did not have the slightest reason to do it. There was no sign of consolation whatsoever in the Archbishop's words. His concept was so new and unusual, that it prompted Father Gherasim to completely forget about his reply and completely focus on the string of Vladika thoughts, to foresee their conclusion. No conclusion could be drawn so far, so the Father decided to wait for the continuation of the monologue.

"Man is made of body and soul. This is commonly known and accepted. In reality, when we look at others, we think of ourselves as being an integral, undivided being, called MAN. Man is neither body nor spirit. It is both these things, together. But not as two separate elements. This is a mystery that the human mind has not yet explained. Man can only be theoretically divided into body and soul. In reality, the two parts are inseparable, like a piece of meat and the cat that had eaten and already digested it. It is practically impossible to determine where the soul ends and where the spirit begins. There are two beginnings: matter and spirit which have fused together. The result of their union is called MAN. The *canker* is undivided as well, and the result of its actions, on the spiritual level, is the regress of the human culture.

"Visualize a painting containing the achievements of the human spirit. Watch it carefully and you will discover the same mark of the same *canker*. It stifles, decays and murders here too. In fact, its marks are even more varied, more numerous, but hardly studied here. When he saw it, Apostle John said: 'For all that is in the world, the lust of the flesh, the lust of the eyes and the pride of life, is not of the Father, but is of the world.' The *canker* is the real reason for the talent downfall of writers. It is guilty of the poor ruling of emperors. It is the enemy of all happiness and joy. Do you understand? Let me give you an example. You are standing in front of the minister, trying to set in motion a well-intended project. You know the minister to be a kind, helpful, receptive person. After looking at your plans, he decides to support them and the future seems bright for you and your project. But your hearing happens to be scheduled exactly when the minister has indigestion, or when he didn't do his siesta, or when he suffers from cataracts, or God knows what. He grumpily greets you and doesn't see anything positive in your project anymore, and with his irritating words, he instantly abolishes your good intention. Also, he transmits his own *canker* to you. Having spoken to him in such moments, you also become irritated and grumpy. All the pessimists in the world are, after all, sick people. Their gloomy theories are nothing more than the result of an abnormal function of their body. If somewhere in a random country the people groan and suffer, or the political and economic situation had worsened, then the explanation must be sought in the mental discrepancies of its leaders, or even in their stomachs. If you listen to a song after which you are overcome with sadness and anxiety, or with the sense of dissatisfaction of an obscure impulse from an undefined distance, you must know that the reason is the mark of the *canker*, marked by a composer already infected. The nostalgic and sad songs of the Russian peasants are the result of a permanent malnutrition, with all the diseases originating from hunger.

"The same happens with literature or the fine arts. Songs for dancing are composed by joyful people. Look at the history of some waltzes that make the young cry, not dance. In most cases, they are the products of some sick authors, who at the time of composing them, were spitting blood.

"Criminals are children of the parents who have been devoured by the same *canker*. In this case, the guilt belongs to one of the countless claws that tear up humanity— alcohol. Such poisons are many. Most of them remain a mystery to scientists, but they're all about the same *canker*.

"The work of the *canker* can easily be observed. For instance, let's take an energetic student, a talented young man, who pleases his parents and teachers with his successes achieved through diligence, inventiveness and good intentions. Deprive him of the fresh air and he becomes anemic or starts to suffer from a sexual disorder. You will see how his mind blunts, his memory weakens, his will vanishes. After a while, he becomes a dull sluggard, being a few steps away from committing a crime. The bad marks for his behavior are also the result of the same *canker*.

"The source of living itself is infected with this *canker*. The healthy instinct of procreation— the commandment *Be fruitful and multiply*— placed at the foundation of happiness, at the hearth of the family life, is also devoured by the same *canker*. Family life had become a living hell for humans. The *canker* acts most consistently here. If in the generations of our great-grandparents and parents the *canker* preponderantly touched the physical, carnal aspect, in the future generations— of our children and grandchildren— the *canker* will produce abortions, prematurely born babies, drying the source and making parents unable to procreate. In the past, the *canker* had attacked particularly the spiritual side of our ancestors' generations, resulting in neurasthenic, psychopathic, epileptic, lunatic, obsessed, idiot descendants or monsters, such as Siamese twins or even veritable freaks who can no longer be called humans. Seeing all this, men became speechless and backed away horrified...

"What is the name of this *canker*? It is nameless. It is known to people under thousands

103

of names, but none of them denounces its complete essence. Its manifestations are called disease or vice. Its experience– pain, torment, tears, cries and moans, troubles. The product of its action is dirtiness, pus, slime, mold, turd. Its reflection in the economic field is poverty, beggary. Its presence in the air, in the water, or in the food is called infection, poison and all that is most toxic. In the sphere of mental activity, its manifestation is known as sin, disgrace, madness, wrongdoing, crime, mistake, and metaphorically – gloom, darkness, the shadow of death, the sleep of death. The purpose of its work is to destroy everything that is alive. It is the final decomposition, the ultimate death of the universe. The result of *canker* upon humans and living beings is called the degeneration towards the finality— death. The *canker* itself has no name. Maybe, the future generations will unveil its secrets, will understand its essence and will give it a name. Today, however, when we speak about it, when we want to give it a generic name, we use the term *evil*.

104

"Alas, this is the enemy to whom you declared war. And you are not the only one fighting it, using all the weapons of science and medicine. The battle is taking place all over the Earth. There are ammunition depots in every town, and now in every village— pharmacies, hospitals, clinics, lazarettos[18]— these all are the main battlefields. Leaders, lawmakers, judges, philosophers, scientists, writers, painters, poets— they are all

---

18 Lazarettos – A war hospital. Term originated probably from Saint Lazarus, the one who was resurrected from the dead by Jesus Christ.

fighting the same enemy. There are thousands and millions of ordinary soldiers, united in brotherhoods, communities, circles. There is an entire army of salvation... But will it truly save mankind from this enemy? If you carefully observe the weapon that people use, you and any other man can guess the answer.

"Presidents and judges have their own weapon— the law. They tell people: *'Do not do this, but do that.'* And then, when a man does something other than what the law commands, he is arrested, flogged and imprisoned. As a result, those who are tortured and beaten object the law: *'We would obey but we cannot!'* Of all the laws, the most rational one is the Law given by God. But even within this Law comes *'the awareness of sin' (Romans 6: 3)*, meaning that whenever the *canker* overwhelms men so much that they cannot distinguish by themselves between good and evil, right or wrong, and their own conscience cannot unveil these to them, then the written law helps them to understand the differences. Apostle Paul said that this law is powerless too, being *'weakened by the flesh' (Romans 8: 3)*, meaning that the *canker* had destroyed men in such a way that they cannot act according to the law anymore. The same Apostle said about himself: *'For I do not do the good I want, but the evil I do not want— this I keep on doing' (Romans 7: 19)*. These words were said almost two thousand years ago, but only now and only partly has society understood that all criminals are basically sick people.

"Philosophers, scientists, researchers... they all want to discover the secrets of the *canker* and help men recognize the enemy. They are like scouts on a battlefield. But their efforts are in vain... the human conscience, defeated by the *canker*, gets tired eventually, going astray, and often repeats its previous mistakes, but under different forms. And even if they manage to recognize the enemy better, that would only bring them halfway. It's not enough to know the enemy; they also must learn how to defeat him.

"What do writers, painters, and poets have in common? They are the ones who inspire the fighters. By exploring the kingdom of the *canker*, they see how men choke in its infested atmosphere and, to save them, they create the ideals of a new life, of a new birth in the kingdom of light, truth, love, beauty, and power. They stir the world towards these ideals, but the people lack the willpower and keep answering with the same words: *'We can't!'* No matter how much you try to motivate a soldier on the battlefield, he will not be able to hold his weapon if both his arms are paralyzed.

"You, Father Gherasim, had seen with your own eyes the powerlessness of the word against the vices of the *asylum inmates*. You had abandoned the word, studied medicine and became a doctor. Indeed, this weapon is more efficient. Since the dawn of this age, men had found hostile powers to the *canker* in the environment and used them to his advantage, healing all sorts of diseases. At first, they cured themselves. Later, specialists appeared, namely all sorts of healers who, in turn, gave their art to medicine and their places to doctors.

"As we know, success for the first time is always exciting and, in this case, the first success was also a great one. Man blindly went to battle against the *canker* but then he came to his senses; he acknowledged that not only can the battle be fought, but it can also be won. Rumors of *the living water, the elixir of life, the philosophical stone* emerged all of a sudden. The young pioneers of natural sciences fervently started to save the world, convincing everybody that it was possible and that if it was not possible then, it was just because science was still too young, and nature had not sufficiently been explored yet. But with the developing of science, some geniuses appeared out of nowhere, offering the world something like the elixir of life that could give strength and energy to the decrepit, helpless and weak man. Once more, humanity shined intensely and healthful, with everlasting beauty and divine spirit. It became immortal.

"Science had abandoned the old utopias when it began to preponderantly make use of experimental methods, learning that all it could offer man was to sustain his life. It could not give him Life. Man is born with a certain amount of vital powers which he consumes during his life and which, once drained, cannot be recovered. He can quickly waste them in his youth or he can thoughtfully preserve them, prolonging his life somehow. This is where medicine really helps. By respecting the rules of hygiene and by using specific medical services, man can stay away from everything that is harmful to his health, therefore lengthening his lifespan. Let's say you have a coat. You can protect it from moths, caringly store it, sew the buttonhole that starts to loosen on time, patch it, and wear it like that all your life, even leave it as an inheritance to your son. But from a shabby, worn-out coat, as yours will eventually become, you cannot make a new one and you cannot have it renewed yearly; instead, it will get used. Things are the same with medicine. The job of the doctors is, in substance, the same: to sew, patch and protect against moths the rusty fleshly shell of the human spirit. In their battle with the *canker*, these soldiers protect the man, snatching him from the claws of the *canker* for a period of time, but the *canker* itself remains intact, invulnerable, while humanity keeps aging more and more."

VIII

ladika bowed his frown head, the shadow of his skufia falling on his face. The lamp, already obscure, got even darker. Father Gherasim stood up, poured some more oil into it and straightened the snuff.

"Behold, this is how the life of mankind fades away as well," continued Vladika after Father Gherasim returned to his place. "According to the Scriptures, the life of the first generations of people lasted for centuries. Many of them lived for almost one thousand years each. But in those times, humans were very vivacious. Even natural sciences agree to that. At the time, the kingdom of *canker* was too weak and had expanded too little. In the time of Noah, however, people's life shortened to one hundred twenty years. This was the maximum length of a human life. The kingdom of *canker* had expanded and had become stronger, covering the entire earth. The Universe itself was in danger of extinction. Everything that contained life was disintegrating, falling to pieces. The vital energies were diminishing. Men began to degenerate. The crown of Creation, the king of nature— man— this wonderful creature, a result of two great sources merging together — matter and spirit— had slowly deteriorated to the brutish behavior and risked to disappear in the same way the mammoths had gone extinct...

"If cholera spreads, people strive to eradicate it as soon as possible. The bed sheets belonging to the infected patient are burned, the room is ventilated, the linings and the clothes are boiled and disinfected through fire and water and various antiseptics preparations. Everything is done to confine the infection and to annihilate its carriers.

"The exact same thing happened to the world. The terrible waters of the Great Flood had purified the Earth. It was a universal cleansing, a worldwide disinfection that, however, had not been performed by man. Everything that had been shattered by the *canker* had been destroyed. The surface of the land soaked by poisonous spores had been disinfected and cleaned, then covered with fruitful mud again. But the *canker* had not been completely destroyed, for it was still present on Noah and his family and on all the living creatures on The Ark. The *canker* had only been weakened.

"If a faithful housewife inspects her wardrobe and notices that one of her dresses is worn-out, she grabs the scissors, cuts out the used parts and creates a skirt for her daughter from the good part of the fabric. So, from a dress, she makes a skirt.

"Man had been created after the flood and would live for one hundred twenty years, thanks to these strong millenary titans, these famous ancient heroes who, in their arrogance, dared to fight the heavens. It's true, Noah himself lived for nine hundred fifty years. He was the strongest, the most durable piece of the fabric from which mankind had been tailored. This is why he was kept. But even after Noah's flood, the years of a man's life rapidly decreased. One hundred twenty years became a rarity. King David already spoke about the years of a man's life to be seventy, eighty at most. But according to the prophet, even the majority of these years are of fruitless labor, sickness, and pain. For the most part of their lifetime, men suffer and struggle.

"We can only but imagine the condition of the world back then. I am not referring here to the Greeks or the Jews who managed to build cities and states, leaving some traces of their culture behind. I am talking about those who scattered throughout the land after the construction of The Tower of Babylon, hiding in forests and caves, whose names have long been forgotten. If it had been possible to achieve such brutish conditions in Sodom and Gomorrah, then what would have happened to those living their lives like animals, surviving in the woods?

"It is said that mankind evolves. In my opinion, the entire life of mankind should be seen as a movement along two curves, starting from the same point and later on split: one goes up and fades in space, the other one descends in bigger or smaller windings.

"Adam is the starting point. Originating from him, mankind has been divided into two camps: one that soared up towards Completion, and the other that soared nowhere, preferring to satisfy its basic instincts and slipping more and more downward, forming a curve that had failed to sustain itself.

"In my opinion, the Greeks made the greatest efforts to perfect and ennoble the human nature. They used to handle the multilateralism and the complexity of man. We can witness the results of the Greek efforts through the plastic art that survived until our time. The statues of Apollo, Venus, Hercules, and others, particularly through the charming beauty of the human face and not just the body shapes, are nevertheless astonishing still to this day. The Greeks wanted to bring the life of the living man into their statues. Their statues do not only reflect the beauty of the body but also of the conscience, the power, the courage, the strength, the audacity, the nobility and all the characteristics of the spirit. The life of humanity has formed a geometric angle whose base side is represented by the man, its ascending side climbs to Apollo, and the other side— to the great-grandfather of today's gibbons. But darkness seized the man, and mankind was in danger of extinction once more. However, it was definitely for the last time."

112

IX

Vladika stopped, somehow exhausted from this long monologue. Father Gherasim was sitting with his head bowed down, feeling the weight of the overwhelming emotions. The nocturnal time was passing quickly. Somewhere, in the distance, some bells struck midnight. Outside, the darkness was getting gloomy and dense, and it looked as though it was romping behind the window, whistling dreadfully. A fierce wave of wind hit the window then rolled away, rattling— the storm was coming.

Father Gherasim remembered his sleepless nights, the torturing memories that, in comparison with the reality that the Archbishop was describing, seemed pale. He realized he had only unveiled a hundredth part of the *canker*. But why was the Archbishop so calm if he had seen its fullness?

Vladika continued as if he guessed the Father's questions:

"The world was dying. It was falling apart. Man, consumed by the *canker*, was quickly degenerating. Mankind had submerged into spiritual poverty so deep that its worthiest representatives, realizing they were standing on the edge of the abyss and nothing could save them anymore, had begun to preach about the ephemeral pleasures, or chose to end their lives, avoiding the suffering and the pain around them. In that moment, voices of Redemption started to emerge; a Redemption that was certain to come soon

"The Jews were the ones who, most distinctly, spoke of it. Prophet Zachariah would preach about *a Spring of Water that would wash away mankind's sins and impurity, opened for the house of David and the inhabitants of Jerusalem (Zachariah 13: 1)*. Prophet Isaiah would express it so clearly like if it had already been an accomplished fact. He would preach about Someone who would take our infirmities upon Himself and would carry our pains. Also, King David would speak of this Someone as *not being corrupted (Psalms 15: 10)*. Speaking of times yet to come, Prophet Isaiah would say what no man would have said at that time: *I am sinful, for the people who will live then, will have all their sins forgiven (Isaiah 33: 24)*. In summary, people would talk of a happening without precedent— the *canker* would be destroyed and its main weapon, depravity, would be reversed. And, indeed, it happened such... The expectations of nations had been fulfilled."

A strange glimmer appeared in the eyes of the Archbishop. He stood up and straightened his back. His gaze floated over Father Gherasim's head, staring somewhere into an invisible distance. It seemed that there, in the deepness

114

of ages, he wanted to disentangle what had really happened and tell the priest about it.

At that moment and in that place, Father Gherasim understood that something was about to happen with him.

Nature itself seemed to have understood it too. In that dilapidated little house, the fate of a soul was about to be decided. Finally, the dead knot which poor Father Gherasim's life had transformed into was going to be cut. Nature acknowledged that and did not refrain itself from casting a lightning on the sleeping earth, followed by the rolling down of the thunder. The lightning burst into the room, illuminating the walls.

Father Gherasim startled involuntarily, but not a single muscle on the Archbishop's face twitched. The superior resumed the conversation, however, not in the modest tone of an ordinary interlocutor, but with the authoritative voice of a preacher echoing the notes of triumphant cheerfulness:

115

"A great, frightening mystery had taken place in one particular spot on earth—in Jerusalem— in the middle of a nation that had astonished the world with its strange history, even prior to that. What exactly happened then will completely remain a mystery. It is said that a great Prophet appeared, one who worked miracles and, with great power, taught the people. He was crucified because, according to the Law of Moses, He was teaching blasphemy. But it had been rumored He had risen from the dead. Some believed it, others doubted it. But all of them began to calm down, after having shuddered in amazement about the happenings. A part of them tried very hard to forget this sad and nonsensical story as soon as possible. However, a small group of people from the apprentices of the murdered Prophet, almost anonymous until then, had separated from the Jews and started living in a special collectivity[19], preaching that the crucified Prophet was none other than the Son of God, equal to God; God Himself..."

"You assume, of course, that I am talking about Christianity," said Vladika, changing his tone. "So strange this teaching dogmatic, don't you think? I believe that if an absolute genius were to create a philosophical system or a teaching inspired by unexplainable mysteries and contradictions, he could not surpass our dogmatic theology. Whatever you might refer to, starting from the Trinitarian Dogma and ending with the little candle in front of the icon, they all contravene a reasonable, healthy, unaltered mind. The most brilliant minds of our theology and philosophy tried to reconcile Christianity with Reason, wasting their talent. All their scholarly works, for which they devoted years and years of hard work, can be instantly shattered by a single tricky question from a *sectarian-muzhik*. Did you have the opportunity to see how our missionaries and theological magistrates despite being armed with all the subtleties of theology and prepared for serious disputes with the rationalist-sectarians, would freeze, incapable of answering a simple

---

19 Collectivity – Christian Jews lived in the first ages unseparated from the Temple and took part in Psalm readings and the Judaic cult, ministering the Lord's Supper (the breaking of bread, the Liturgy) only in private houses. The beginning of their separation from the Temple happened when Archdeacon Stephan was killed by the Jews.

question born in the childish mind of a muzhik? Not to mention in front of the representatives of natural sciences. To them, Christianity is so contradictory that they have ceased to talk about it altogether. Then there are some genius minds, like our Leo Tolstoy, who refuse to part entirely from Christianity, but they canceled the dogma, arguing that it was invented by the *people*, *(a.n.* to be read– *hierarchs)* and that Christ Himself did not mention anything alike. This is not true! There are no additional words in our dogma. It represents the exquisite revelation of the true teachings of the Apostles, who have accurately passed on the words of the Savior. If Christianity is considered contradictory nowadays, in ancient times, people used much tougher terms: they called it *insanity*, meaning opposite to reason. But in spite of this contradiction, Christianity had been received by people and had spread almost all over the world, counting its already twentieth century.

117

"The nature of these things would seem enigmatic to many people. But in fact, they are much simpler. Do we accept in our lives only what our mind can understand? More often than not, we do the exact opposite: we accept that which is totally incomprehensible. For years, Columbus tried to prove the existence of a new continent to Europeans, but nobody believed him. Only after he sailed there and returned with the proof did the people accept his ideas. Mostly, they didn't have any other choice. Tell an old peasant woman that steam can pull a carriage faster than a horse. Would she believe you? No, but once a railway station has been built inside the village and the woman rides on the train, she agrees that steam can transport people, even though she doesn't understand how. Do people know how what electricity is? Or how was the telephone invented? No, but that doesn't prevent them from using the telephone, the telegraph or to admit the existence of electricity. In this case, the real fact is presented– this can be perplexing, it can somehow be explained, but definitely it cannot be denied.

"People did not deny Christianity from its very beginnings because of similar reasons. The preaching of the Apostles was strange and puzzling, but the happening was real and people accepted Christianity. What were the Apostles preaching? Firstly, they weren't preaching or teaching anything in the sense of what these terms mean today. They would simply travel and spread the good news, the happenings in Jerusalem, to the entire world. What did really happen according to them? *And this is the Life that was revealed; for we have seen it and testified to it, and we proclaim to you the eternal Life that was with the Father and was revealed to us (1 John 1: 2).* What was subject to corruption became incorrupt, and the mortal flesh— immortal. Behold, the essence of the Gospel, of the good news. This is the quintessence of their preaching. Speaking of it, the Apostles said about themselves: *We were taught to put off our former way of life, our old self, which is being corrupted by its deceitful desires; to be renewed in the spirit of our minds; and to put on the new self, created to be like God in true righteousness and holiness (Ephesians 4: 22–24). We have already passed from death to life (John 1: 3-14) and, even though we still sigh waiting for the redemption of our bodies (Romans 8: 23), our old self-rots, while our new self-renews day by day.* Have you ever seen how the tree bulbs flourish? The germ of the new fruit sprouts on the inside, while on the outside, the fruit starts to putrefy. The layer of the fruit rots and is gradually replaced with a new one. Dig up a half rotten onion planted in the spring and you would hold a completely new onion in your hand by autumn.

"This was what the listeners were understanding from the apostolic preaching. People kept listening and saw that the Apostles were, indeed, some kind of beings from whom life was gushing like a spring: very energetic, uncommonly courageous in spirit, with an extraordinarily sharp mind that could predict the future, beings who would not feel pain, but instead would emit energies so powerful that the sick would heal only by touching their clothes. These people would not fear death at all. If they would have drunk any poisonous liquid, they would not have been harmed. The difference between the preachers of Christianity and other people was so striking that, at Lystra, after seeing Paul and Varnava, the pagans said: 'They are the descended gods in human form,' and Zeus priests hurried to present them offerings. It took the Apostles a lot of work to convince the people that they were not gods but ordinary men.

"Back then, the people who wanted to be like the Apostles would ask: 'What must we do to be like thy?' And they would receive the answer: 'First, abandon your old way of living and live as we do, be baptized in the Name of Jesus Christ, then do this and that and you'll see for yourselves

119

how you will be reborn like us. For Christ said: *And these signs shall follow those who believe; in my Name, they shall cast out devils; they shall speak with new tongues; they shall take up serpents; and if they drink any deadly thing, it shall not hurt them; they shall lay hands on the sick, and they shall recover (Mark 16: 17 18)*. And people would do what they were told, becoming like the Apostles, giving praise to the Crucified Prophet and naming Him God. And like that, Christianity would spread all over the world."

Vladika stopped talking, meditated a few seconds, then continued:

"By the way, here is a question: Is Christ really God? This is such a difficult question to many that, unable to find an answer to it, they stopped assigning Jesus Christ the title of God, calling Him only a Holy Teacher or an unusual Man. People said that the Apostles were wrong in believing their Teacher to be God Himself, all the more since even He never spoke of Himself in that way. I do not agree. What is so hard to understand here?! Anyway, what is God?

"Being born on Earth, Christ named himself Life, meaning God. Could have his disciples honored him like that? Let's take an example. What is a doctor? A person who heals. If a man comes to your home and says: 'I am a doctor,' will you believe him? Maybe yes, maybe not. But if you are sick in bed and a stranger comes and visits you, brings with him medication, starts taking care of you and, in the end, heals you, I presume you will name him doctor even if he doesn't think of himself like one.

"When Christ was living among his disciples making miracles, and moreover, passing this power unto them too, the Apostles never thought of naming him God. Only Peter, in an enthusiastic burst of affection towards the Teacher, called Him the Son of God. But shortly after, he revoked his statement because he was afraid of the Jews. But when they felt the Life starting to vigorously spring within them, when they saw that a new power had revived within their souls, transforming them into new people, when they understood that this was, in fact, the fulfillment that the Teacher had promised to give them, they didn't hesitate to call Him Life, meaning God. They believed then in His Resurrection, in the same Resurrection they didn't previously believe when He appeared in front of them after His death. So they told the world: *'Life was revealed and we have seen it, we testify and we proclaim it to you.'* Neither the fear of the Jews nor the torments and tortures they were subjected to by countless persecutors, had prompted them to give up Life.

"The first preachers of Christianity were followed by a large number of people; martyrs, witnesses, hierarchs, hermits, whose names fill our Synaxaria. They were strong men, solid in body and spirit, with abilities of the soul that people had no idea of until then. They knew, for example, secrets of the human language and they could understand or speak in foreign languages. They could read other people's minds; they could communicate at great distances between them in a way hidden from us. In a nutshell, they were new men indeed, new *beings* in Christ. But so viable they were! Do you know what viability means? Cut a lizard's tail and cast it aside. After wandering a bit, the lizard finds its tail, stick its body to it, and the tails will glue back to its body right under your eyes. And if it doesn't find it, then the lizard will regenerate a new one. The ability of the body to regenerate its damaged tissues is called viability.

"The contemporary man has almost lost this viability completely. His body is nothing more but an old decaying junk, falling apart at the first stroke. Think of all the effort and time it needs just to heal an injury or repair tissues damaged by diseases! Even after recovering its daily loses through food and rest, man still feels a permanent deficit. Even if he recovers his strength, he will always do it with deficiency; sometimes more significant, other times less. In the end, the sum of these deficiencies will lead to a complete failure. Man becomes a helpless, sad, weak, incapable being. Metaphorically, he becomes a vegetable, a mackerel, a piece of cloth. In reality, he turns into a corpse.

"We notice something entirely unusual about the first Christians. They were remarkably viable. For instance, take the ascetic Christians from Thebaid and other deserted regions. Not only did they not take care of their body, but they seemed to be doing the exact opposite, something that others would call self-destruction; they would labor themselves while fasting, they would spend their time doing interminable work, they would consume the most meager meals possible in very limited quantity, they would dwell wherever they could find shelter– in caves, in holes, cellars, and they would cover their bodies in rags. Not only did

122

their strength not weaken, but on the contrary, their inner being had renewed itself daily. With every passing day, they gain a surplus of energy and no deficits. They had so much strength, energy, and life that, not knowing what to do with all of it, some of them would hang heavy metal rings on their uncovered bodies, would tie their legs with iron chains, would bury themselves up to their neck in the ground, would climb really tall pillars and would lay there for 40 days. As a result, they would have a long and painless old age. All ascetics lived very long lives, after which they would fall asleep rather than die.

"I've almost forgotten one detail. Remember when I was telling you about how people try in various ways to hide the awful smell that characterizes them? Well, the ascetics of the deserts did not care at all about this, and would not try to smell nice. They didn't tolerate scents or soaps. Many of them would not bathe, would not shower, would not change their clothes in years but, no matter how strange it may seem, they didn't smell bad at all. What is more, towards the end of their lives, their bodies started emanating a fine scent of rose.

"Behold what Christianity has done and still does. It defeated the hidden root of what we call *canker* and destroyed it from within people and the world. A major turning point has been produced in the life of mankind when Christianity came into the world. From the last position of the descending curve, mankind stopped slipping and reverted back to the ascending curve. This ascending curve goes far away into an endless rise, piercing the sky. So long and captivating is this perspective! By passing from degeneration to rebirth, mankind will succeed, as Apostle Paul said, *in merging his coarse, perishable body, with the glorious Body of Christ (Philippians 3: 21).*

"Can you visualize the evangelical Image of Christ? Transpose your mind to Mount Tabor. *His face was shining like the sun and His clothes were as white as snow…* These are the first steps that the darkened body has to take towards the staircase of rebirth, of illumination. Any man shines, but with a dark and ugly light, invisible to our eyes. That light that can rarely be seen on the graves of the dead when the rotting of the corpse amplifies. In fact, it is the result of degradation. The decaying wood in the forest shines the same light at night. The first sign of a man's rebirth is the absence of this radiation, initially achieved by weakening then complete destroying the impurity in man. By liberating itself from impurity, the body achieves the ability to illuminate with a different glimmering, especially during praying, a brighter one, which, in time, turns into a real brilliance. But this isn't a finality either…"

"Please, forgive me, Vladika, may I ask you a question?" intervened Father Gherasim. "What can we do in order to obtain such life powers, maybe not like the Apostles, but at least like the ascetics you mentioned? Did we not receive the same baptism?"

"Baptism is but the first step. It only cleanses. We shall talk about what it cleanses when the time comes. Baptism, however, doesn't give life. Then what is it that gives man life and how is this life maintained? Food and water. If you do not eat for a couple of weeks, you'll die.

124

Through his digestive system, man extracts from food and water the necessary substances to maintain his life, to replenish the daily amount of lost energy, and to restore damaged tissues. But as I was telling you, expenses always surpass incomes, and, in the end, this deficit leads to failure. If things were different, then man would never degenerate. Remember the debate our Savior had with the Jews after the extraordinary feeding of the people with five loaves of bread? In this conversation, Christ explained to them that this deficit takes place because the food that the people were eating was also perishable, even the wonderful bread given to them in the desert– the manna from heaven– and which, due to its marvelous properties, their ancestors called it the bread of the angels. By saying this, The Savior told the Jewish people that He would offer them the unalterable, living, life-giving bread, and real food and real drink. Then He clearly and unambiguously told them that this bread was His body and the drink was His blood, leaving no room for any symbolic interpretation of these words. So, the ones who understood the true sense of these words and received this food became just like the Apostles."

125

"You are referring to the Holly Eucharistic Sacrament. But, Vladika, don't we receive the Eucharist?" asked Father Gherasim, betraying a certain sadness in his voice.

Vladika pretended not to hear the question. He stood up, straightened his stiff limbs and, slowly crossing the room, stopped in front of the cabinet where Father Gherasim kept his medicines.

"What do you have in here?" he asked, pointing to one of the little bottles.

"Quinine, Vladika," answered the Father confused.

"Medicine against fever... How often must one take it per day and for how many days?"

"Three, four times a day, depending on the gravity of the illness. One should take it until the fever breaks down."

"Therefore, one must take this medicine three or four times a day and pay the doctor a few visits, in order to get rid of fever. Do the same with the Great Medicine that our Lord gave us. The Apostles and the first Christians would receive the Eucharist daily, spending their time in love and continuous praying. And we, the haters, the flatterers, who are always ready to trip someone, come to our Heavenly Doctor once a year and demand immediate cure from all diseases, distresses and sufferings inherited from our ancestors... We expect nature, which had deteriorated over thousands of years, to instantly revive, and we to become new people. But do we really want it? Are we going to show up to the Holy Communion with such thoughts? In my youth, I once saw an officer of the regimental guard entering the church, bewilderedly walking around, waving his whip and asking where he could receive Communion. When I revoltingly asked him why an unbeliever wanted to receive the Eucharist, he answered with a pure soldierly courtesy: 'You see, I need a certificate which proves I was present at Confession and Communion... In accordance with my job... My

126

superiors constrain me... Would you be so kind and explain to me how this is done?'

"So, first of all, *a requirement for the certificate.* In this case, of course, no Sacrament occurs. It is only blasphemy! Such an attitude towards the Communion had the Corinthians too whom Apostle Paul scolded: 'This is why many are sick and ill among you, and many have died.'"

It was already raining outside. Large drops of water were falling and trickling in transparent stripes on the window. The morning chill filled the shack. Sitting next to the window, Father Gherasim felt a shudder through his body.

"God"—he thought— "I feel now how the forces of nature are acting upon me. Why can't I perceive the action of the godly power in the same clear and distinct way? The Grace that is so often spoken of in Christianity? Vladika says it is enough to come to Christ and everything will become clear... Vladika doesn't understand me. He can't imagine how deep the worm of doubt has penetrated my soul, for I find it difficult to take even the first step. How can I think that, by standing in front of the Holy Table, God's Grace acts within me by ordination if I don't truly sense it? How can I open my eyes so that they can see the true Flesh and Blood of Christ, instead of bread and wine? It is a mystery. Of course, if this is true, it must be a great mystery, beyond the understanding of the human mind. But how can one convince himself that it is a great mystery and not a deception? That it is really something enigmatic?! Because it is possible to be nothing else but only what the eyes can see... I don't demand complete knowledge but only the smallest proof, so that my mind could grasp it... The rest I could believe..."

Father Gherasim decided to go all the way, confessing his thoughts to the Archbishop. Vladika listened, then answered thoughtfully:

"The Sacrament of Eucharist is impenetrable. However, if it is truly a mystery, if it comprises in itself something too great to be accessible, if it is difficult for the human mind to comprehend it, we can only find out by experimenting. I suggest you make an introspection on your own self as well as on your parishioners, those unfortunate inmates from the asylum. You have acted by word, by your personal example, and by charity, but in the end, you've come to the same negative result. What is more, while you were teaching others, you found yourself on the verge of falling in the pit. Listen to my advice now. Place both yourself and your parishioners under the uninterrupted work of the Holy Sacraments and you will see a reversed effect that can only be sensed by the mind.

"There are many things that allow Christianity to be received not only by faith but also by proof. But the problem here is different ... In fact, I don't understand what kind of obstacles reason can place on faith. Reason alone knows nothing about all this. Our natural science is nothing more than a mere farmer boy that praises his parents' shack and is skeptical about the existence of palaces described by a guest from the city. He has no clue that the palace is nothing more than another level of improvement for his shack.

"In general, I don't understand the sense of these contradictions between faith and knowledge, between religion and reason. It is just an artificially problem inflated partly by ignorance, partly by bad intention. Science expresses what is explored and known while faith implies the unknown and unexplored. That's all there is to it. What kind of contradiction do you see here?

Father Gherasim remained silent. Everything the Archbishop had told him was new. Indeed, he had never paid any attention to them. Until now. The Father used to minister the Sacrament of Baptism the same way as other clergymen in town, thinking that it was just a symbolic act in memory of Jesus Christ's Baptism in the Jordan River. But did he think like this only about Baptism? He thought of many sermons to be simple rituals, some of them said to intensify the state of praying, while others were totally meaningless.

However, now... what now? The Father's thoughts were tangling. He felt something overwhelming his chest. He wanted to shout, not out of pain but out of joy: "Lord, it means You didn't abandon the world! It means Your power is still here! It means everything is still possible!"

"Dear Father Gherasim!" exclaimed the Archbishop unexpectedly. "Cast aside your doubt! Remember your poor parishioners. Remember they are dying. I know you cherish them but you were about to die as well, hoping that, in your ignorance, you could have saved them by yourself. Now you have learned that nothing is possible without Christ and that His saving power is still working in this world. Embrace this power and begin your work again. Bring it to completion. From now on, your work will be much easier."

129

The Father agreed his work will be easier now because he could see the hope, a strong and brilliant hope, standing in front of him. For him, life got brighter from a different perspective. He joyfully stood up and, with serene eyes, he looked at the Archbishop. Vladika replied back with a calm and warm gaze, after which he stood up too.

The first light of dawn was breaking. The oil in the lamp was burning out, but the morning light was illuminating the room.

Vladika looked at Father Gherasim and could hardly recognize the same priest from the church. So much has the expression on his face changed. The Archbishop's vigilance caught, however, a shadow of sadness and concern that darkened the priest's forehead.

"What is it now? What troubles you?"

The Father's gaze faded.

"Your Holiness," he murmured. "I..."

Father Gherasim stopped. The words could not reach his tongue.

"Go on," said Vladika calmly and authoritatively at the same time.

"Your Holiness, I am a sinner... I am not a priest... I wasn't..."

"I know. You were a teacher. You taught people the evangelical truths. Any Christian, lecturer or professor can do this. When you were helping the poor, healing the sick, and sharing their sufferings, you were a humanist. When you were burying the dead you were a churchman, a ritualistic, but you were not a reviver, a sanctifier, a priest. What good does recalling this do now? *And your sins shall not be mentioned*, said God. In the throes of doubt, you have fallen into desperation and consciously walked away from Christ. Your conscience is bothering you now, but there is a remedy for this as well— the Holy Confession. You have already confessed to me. Therefore, receive forgiveness.

May our Lord and God, Jesus Christ, with His Grace and the plenty fullness of His gifts, with His love for mankind, forgive you, my son, all your transgressions..."

Father Gherasim dropped down, piously kneeling in front of his Archbishop. Vladika made the sign of the cross on himself, and since he did not bring the epitrachelion with him, he placed the edges of his cassock on the Father's head and carried on with the prayer:

"And I, His unworthy archbishop, through the power invested in me given by Him, forgive and absolve you from all your sins, in the Name of the Father, and of the Son, and of the Holy Spirit. Amen..."

The Father quietly stood up and, full of joy, he kissed the hand of the one who blessed him.

"Look, the dawn is breaking!" Vladika pointed to the window. "May this be the dawn of a new and bright life to you as well. Look, the sun is rising soon. What a beauty indeed!"

Vladika went to the window. The Father's house was close to the outskirts of the town. There was no field after the courtyard which the window was facing towards to prop the horizon illuminated by the light of the dawn. The first golden rays entered the room and, shortly after, the sun made its majestic and serene appearance in all the splendor of its brilliance.

131

"Well now, we should be heading to our home," said Vladika.

He grabbed his staff and prayed in front of the icons. Father Gherasim put his hat on and opened the door for the Archbishop.

132

X

he petty merchant women rushing to the market opened their sleepy eyes wide when they spotted the Archbishop walking so naturally in the street. They stopped and stared at him for a long time, marveling at this unlikely scene. The clever ones put down their things and rushed towards him, asking for a blessing.

Vladika was lively walking and rhythmically hitting the pavement with his staff, joyfully inhaling the morning air. He was curiously observing the sleeping town and cheerfully exchanging a word or two with Father Gherasim every now and then. His face was radiating of freshness, with no signs of a sleepless night.

The town was sleeping, but many people were wandering in the streets. Most of them were thin and covered in rags.

"Are they your parishioners?" asked Vladika.

"Yes... They came to check out the streets..."

"You have quite a lot of them... I've never seen anywhere so many. Your parish is too big. You need help. This is what we will do. I must talk to you about your parish, so please visit me this evening. By the way, could you gather all these people in the church someday?"

"Why not? I must try..."

"If you succeed, please let me know. I will come. I wish to talk to them. Behold, we're home already... For now, see you soon! Go and rest. God bless you.

XI

assing by the surprised doorman, Vladika nimbly walked up the stairs of the bishop house, heading to his office. He threw his coat aside and sat energetically at the writing table.

Here, however, he lost his liveliness. Suddenly, his arms fell helplessly on the soft edges of the armchair, his look frowned, his eyes faded and his face darkened. But this was not the effect of a sleepless night. Those nights had been many in the Archbishop's life and they all passed without leaving any trace.

Vladika was thinking about the conclusions of his visit.

"It's the same everywhere, be it this or any other eparchy. Father Gherasim is the only surprising and big exception. This priest who calls himself an atheist is, in fact, a spiritual titan, defeated not by a mountain but by a stick, by a monster that calls itself contemporary theology, snatching the ground from under his feet. But now, he rose back up... the impulse has

135

been given. He will continue his journey alone. He will reveal the world the true Christian within him unless the world won't break him first. The people want real shepherds, and if they will recognize such a shepherd in Father Gherasim, they will immediately proclaim him a saint, excluding him from his environment. They will place him on a pedestal and worship him like they did with another shepherd of ours[20], putting an end to this entire story. For as long as good people dwell among us, we are full of remorse and uncomfortable around them, because their image forces us to aspire to similar values. And we strive to follow them, to imitate them, no matter how little. However, for everything to fall apart, it is enough to declare a good man to be a saint.

"We quickly try to get rid of this *obligation to aspire* and replace it with worshiping; the saint is put on a pedestal, under the pedestal a tin can, and in the thin can people throw their coins. This is what everything has been reduced to. And for instructing the people, a book is written about the saint's *life* in which, with an extreme effort, are gathered the most unusual events of his life, the most astonishing miracles that he performed in order to make the saint look as holy as possible and very different from ordinary people. In this way, people forget that the saint himself was a simple man like them and that, by respecting the proportions, they too could become like him.

"People believe it is feasible to transmit anything through inheritance to their successors:

---

20 Shepherd of ours – An allusion to St. John of Kroonstad.

wealth, title, rank, even the bodily and spiritual abilities like character and talents. They made an exception regarding one thing only: they believe that the holy characteristics of the spirit and the body cannot be hereditarily transmitted. The work of Salvation has been crammed in the tiny orifice of each individual's *moral completion*.

"There is no experience from past generations. Each individual must act alone and, moreover, start from the beginning each time. Because of this, we don't have experienced leaders. Priests? Oh, how little I fancy all these *fair and clean little priests*, with their carefully-ironed skufias, with all their crosses and long service decorations, who strictly obey all regulations and prescriptions! They are the most dangerous enemies of Christianity. Priesthood is an art. What would have happened with our literature if all the writers would have strictly followed the rules of literature? They would have written syllabic verses until today. The authentic priesthood, like art, cannot be systematized. Indeed, it is better to have to deal with priests like Father Paul than with these *honest clerks*. By the way, I mustn't forget. I absolutely must assign Father Paul in the eparchy. He is the most proper priest to help Father Gherasim. They complete each other..."

His thoughts returned to Father Gherasim again.

"Now, it depends on how the seeds will sprout within him. These steps will be the first for me too in this new eparchy. O Lord! Please, do not deprive us of Your blessing...!

"We must hurry. We must light the fire of Christianity, show it to the people, and then

137

preach it... Better sooner than later... As soon as possible... Although, haste can be harmful to success. O, Lord! Deliver us from the temptation— the great temptation — in which Your faithful servants fell, in which Pharisees and Scribes crucified You, afraid that the people's belief might fall, afraid that they might break Your commandments given through Moses. Deliver us from this temptation— from the fear of carrying Your work in the world. It is so simple and easy to fall into such a temptation, to shift from worker to keeper, then to administrator and, in the end, to consider yourself the master...! Then, whoever will disagree with your opinion will be seen as an enemy of God, and in an outburst of holy zeal, you'll crucify him... Oh Lord, Oh Lord! Let not our will but Yours be done... Just be with us until the end... Save us..."

138

Vladika leaned back in his armchair, stretched out his legs and, by placing his hands crossed on his chest, he fell asleep. He was dead tired. His closed eyes and his calm breathing confirmed that Vladika was now deeply asleep.

But an hour later, after washing his face and chest with cold, fresh water, and reading his morning prayers, Vladika sat down at his writing table with the intention to start working. He grabbed a thick folder from the table, brought by his secretary, that contained different requests, reports, and protocols. But after signing a few of them, he dropped the quill pen and quickly stood up.

"What a pity... they have clothed the living work of Christ, to Satan's delight, in protocols, documents, and journals. They flooded the

Episcopal chanceries with paperwork, distracting bishops from their real mission. Sadly, they succeeded, for bishops no longer have time to work among their flock... but no more! In the Name of our Lord Jesus Christ, we will still fight Satan. Stay here, you little ones, right here."

Vladika set aside the stack of papers and covered it with a huge paperweight.

"No big loss... A complaint file from the parishioners against their priest. This trial of reciprocal insults lasted for three years... one hundred fifty paper sheets... it takes three hours just to read it. I've even seen the priest and his parishioners recently; they showed up here, together, to solve some issues for a school opening festival. They all have long forgotten about the complaint. But I sit here writing resolutions only because the file is next in line... Enough! I shall focus on something better..."

Vladika called his apprentice and ordered him to contact the economos priest from the eparchial house.

A few minutes later, the economos priest was already receiving his blessings from the Archbishop.

"Father economos! I heard that there is an archbishop villa somewhere in the suburbs."

"There is, Your Grace!"

"Is it big?"

"The building is enormous – plus the outhouses, the garden, the lake, three acres of forest, and about two acres of land."

"Who owns the neighboring land?"

"The town, Your Grace."

"Is it still available? Is it much?"

139

"They lease it for pasture... it's a large area. About 100 deseatines[21]"

"Well look, here's what we will do. The villa is too small for me. Please, take the carriage and go to the mayor. Ask him, in my name, if he will sell the land and at what price. If he won't sell it, then ask him to lease it to us for a long term. If not all of it, at least about twenty deseatines. Did you understand? Well, hurry up then..."

"Understood, Your Grace. Just that... allow me to report: Wouldn't you like to first inspect the villa personally? Maybe it isn't worth buying the land. The other archbishops were satisfied with it..."

"No, no. I told you it's too tight for me there. Five deseatines is too little."

"But with what resources, Your Grace?"

"Well, this is not your concern anymore, is it? Now, go!"

The economos priest walked away perplexed, trying to satisfy Vladika's *caprice*.

140

XII

In no time, all those connected whatsoever with the eparchial house were speaking only about the Archbishop's actions. They were judging, sharing their opinion, and making assumptions. The gossips never seemed to end since Vladika gave them every day new and new reasons to continue. The spiciest conversations were those related to the Archbishop's new concept for the household. Vladika started to rebuild the eparchial house. Carpenters, builders, stove fitters, all were swarming inside the rooms... the economos priest could hardly fulfill the Archbishop's instructions.

Not so much the fact that the house was being rebuilt, but the manner in which it was done—this is what concerned the eparchial personnel. All the rooms were taking the shape of a labyrinth composed of many small chambers.

"He is ruining the palace," mumbled the economos priest. "What has gotten into him?"

"Maybe he's thinking of a hotel..." Anton, the coachman, asked himself, thoroughly meditating. "But who is he going to accommodate in it? Does he really have so many relatives?"

"Many, my dear Anton, many," the Archbishop, who was just passing by and heard his monologue, patted him on the shoulder.

"But he said he didn't have any relatives..." the coachmen, a little confused, finished his thought while going down the stairs.

Soon, however, everything had been clarified. The economos priest to whom Vladika had presented his projects explained Piotr Akimîci the following:

"Well, this is all for the priests who are coming to visit us. Vladika said that he is a hierarch, the Father of all priests, and he wants them to come to him as the sons come to their fathers."

The economos priest explained the Archbishop's idea very accurately— the hierarch set his mind to provoke a closeness not only between priests but also between priests and their bishop. This was his biggest dream. As a son of a provincial priest and with knowledge of the life and habits of the rural clergy, Vladika knew that nothing could bring the priests closer than the meetings at various inns or hotels where the priesthood would gather for different reunions or occasions, or at school openings. They could talk wholeheartedly to one another here, not in the meeting halls. So, the hotel, not the eparchial house, became the actual link that unified everybody as a whole. This was a powerful instrument for getting closer to his flock, and Vladika intended to use it to its full potential.

The innovation lacked any trace of artificiality or obligations, which is why it surpassed all the Archbishop's expectations. Accustomed to simplicity, the priests from the countryside felt really comfortable finding the same simplicity inside the eparchial house. They preferred to stay here because it would be cheaper than a hotel at least.

The eparchial house took on an unusual appearance. At times, it resembled an ant-hill. Many priests, deacons, and readers came here by carriage or walk, carrying their handbags.

At the entrance, the same Akimîci received them. He was no longer the old and stately doorman, with a parade tunic, bowing only to town priests and neglecting the village ones. Piotr Akimîci simply became Akimîci, a gentle and merry old man, who would greet the Archbishop's guests with great bustle. The elder and poorer the priest was, the more attentive and caring Akimîci became; he immediately received the blessing and, after snatching the priest's suitcase, he walked the Father all the way to the little room where he was accommodated.

The cold and harsh walls of the bishop's house where only the properly combed and dressed priests used to come, with their skufias and their Cross correctly arranged, with the indispensable *report* in their hand, were now emanating warmth and light. The joys, the troubles, the sufferings, the happiness, they all began to flow like a river in this place. Here, under the wise guidance of the Archbishop, all of life's impulses found meaning and direction and were touched by the spirit of evangelical teaching; by filling themselves with

143

benevolence and Christian love, the priests traveled to all corners of the eparchy, spreading further the same spirit of kindness and affection.

Slowly and unexpectedly, the clergy gathered around the Archbishop forming a large and close family, held together by the same spirit and curdled by the same will.

The chancellor office became speechless. Rarely did any papers arrive here anymore apart from those unavoidable; such as tax invoices. They were paid and sent to the archive whereas the real important things were decided at a cup of tea, particularly in the evenings, after the priests had solved their matters in town, and had returned to visit their Archbishop. He greeted them in a large hall loaded with many tables, on top of which samovars were boiling.

Reports were forgotten as well. They were replaced by live conversations that sometimes lasted long after midnight.

In the meantime, since Vladika would not use any other transportation means apart from the tram and walks, the bishop's carriage had been covered with a thick layer of dust.

The stable suffered some radical adjustments too. It was transformed into a long row of stable bars, separating the horses, where the countryside priests could leave their jades.

The town priests did not comply with the new eparchial order as easily and devotedly as those from the rural area. The *townspeople* had managed to absorb and assert their own urban conventions, giving in to the toils of conduct rules, of conservative and official politeness that created, although honorable, an unbearably suffocating atmosphere for the villagers.

The simplicity of the Archbishop shocked this part of the clergy, for they liked to measure their position according to military ranks and had a special satisfaction whenever their counterpart in the military hierarchy is one hell of a *colonel*. These *spiritual people* liked having a boss who would not give in to the governor. They were very displeased with humble archbishops and would think of them as *little bishops* who lower the clergy's prestige in the eyes of the high society. Initially, Vladika's request to be *randomly* visited and *without any reason* was met with enthusiasm by the priesthood, including the clerical figures. It was very pleasant to visit an important figure for no reason.

But even from the very first cup of tea in the Archbishop's house, the townspeople realized that these simple get-together visits were constraining them to a behavior beyond their powers. This meant that they had to act according to the true virtue of humility, even towards the last village priest, and not fake a formal equality. They had to forget their positions and ranks, to abandon their titles, and be who they truly were. The clerical figures got upset. However, on the outside, they showed submission because, even though the new Vladika had an excessively modest behavior, he was not at all a *little archbishop*. They felt the strength in him.

Instead, a circle of priests, who had not yet got sucked into the quotidian mud of conventions, began to gather rapidly around the new Vladika. The heart and soul of this circle were Father

Grigori and Father Gherasim, who quickly became friends. This happened in the following manner: one evening, Father Grigori gave up waiting for the Archbishop and headed towards the eparchial palace himself.

He saw many priests there, including Father Gherasim. The presence of Father Gherasim amazed Father Grigori for he knew his friend's *pixilated* attitude towards archbishops. The archbishop hall was echoing with voice; more or less spicy conversations were held everywhere. Vladika himself was speaking with half of his voice, explaining something to Father Gherasim.

At the right moment, Father Grigori drew the Archbishop's attention and started talking about the moral and religious situation of the town.

Father Grigori expected Vladika to answer with the highest sympathy towards the downfall of religiosity in society. To his great surprise, he noticed that the Archbishop was not paying too much attention to his discourse and, in some moments, he even gave him funny but kind looks. The Father didn't like that. He considered, and for good reason, that such a serious matter required an equally serious attitude. Jokes did not belong there. And if Vladika was joking, that meant he did not understand the great danger hanging over religion.

Father Grigori lost his calm tone and, visibly nervous, made a remark to Vladika:

"Your Grace, we are living in harsh times. Our society is experiencing a crisis of religious consciousness. One must be naïve not to notice the dangers threatening religion. Now, every moment, every minute is precious. If the

146

priesthood misses this chance, it will become an eyewitness to the total destruction of religion. Religion is already declining amongst people."

"Let it decline! Let it decline!" answered Vladika, in the same humorous tone.

Father Grigori stared at the Archbishop with his eyes wide open. The smile suddenly disappeared from Vladika's face:

"Religiosity is declining – praised be the Lord! The sooner the better! And it will decline, for the Lord is mighty and has not abandoned Russia yet. The Holy Orthodox faith will be born in this country once more…"

"I understand from your words, Your Grace, that you make an important distinction between religion and faith. What is this dissimilarity?" asked Father Grigori bewildered. Vladika returned to his joking tone:

"Well, faith is when you say *let me give you a small icon for the road*, and religion, *in honor of such thing or in memory of such event, a shrine has been arranged in such place…* Just think about it; why were icons representing the same saint hanged in all the train stations and state institutions at some point in time? Find the answer to this question and you'll discover the difference between religion and faith…"

The Father understood the Archbishop's allusion and grew thoughtfully.

"And this word, *religion*, doesn't seem a proper one to me," continued Vladika. "It's not a Christian word. It is a pagan term and it brought pagan elements to Christianity. And as for faith, no need to feel sad," added the Archbishop, noticing the concerned expression

147

on the Father's face. "Think more of the Divine Providence. We state that we are led by God's Spirit. Our fear of God's work in the world is the result of our own torpor. Be more lively! Work more joyfully and cast away temptations. Work in your parish, but work together, helping each other and sharing the experience. Look, you could help Father Gherasim in organizing his parish. Father Gherasim,"—Vladika turned to the priest— "update Father Grigori with your mission. He has wealthy parishioners and can attract the necessary investments and, as a result, the material aspect of the problem will be solved. In fact, you should make the preparations starting from tomorrow. We already have the land; the town hall will donate it. You can use my summer villa, including the church there, for the time being. Father Paul will be a helpful hand. I'm glad you are old friends... I'm listening," Vladika turned towards a priest from the countryside, grabbed hold of his arm and walked away together. The priest started to tell him something, gesturing energetically.

148

Father Gherasim began to update his colleague about the *enterprise* mentioned by the Archbishop. He explained to him everything in detail, including the memorable discussion he had with the hierarch, in that memorable night, until the break of dawn.

The atmosphere in the archbishop hall, the words of the Archbishop, the lively story of Father Gherasim regarding the *business*, were emanating a flow of vivacity, freshness, and joy. Father Grigori embraced this new flow with all his being.

XIII

ather Gherasim needed a considerable amount of effort to gather all the town ruffians in his church. If it hadn't been for the volunteers from the asylums who decided to help their parish priest, probably nothing would have come out of it. An important fact was that all the vagabonds had personally known Father Gherasim, and some were nourishing a feeling of admiration towards the priest. They strived to show him signs of gratitude on different occasions. They agreed to gather in the church on a specific day, mostly out of respect for the Father.

149

The most concerned of all was Fedotici. He scoured the entire town, visited all the asylums, searched all the corners where he believed to find asylum candidates, asking them to immediately show up at Father Gherasim's church.

Finally, the Father announced to his Archbishop that the preparations had been made.

On that day, Father Gherasim's church was an unusual sight to see. Numerous ragged, down-at-heel people, beggars, infirm men, and women, from all corners of the town, were dragging themselves to the church. Some were high and mighty and kept holding their heads up, giving scornful looks to the public. Others were airily waving their threadbare canes, occasionally accosting passers-by with the same humble request: 'Mate, a small loan, please, to a former student for the *hotel*!' Others, afraid of the daylight, preferred to come through dark alleys. But all in all, the majority were walking round-shouldered, stumbling along and observing the people around with dim and impassive gazes.

After entering the church, some started to gather in small groups, while the lonely withdrew into the corners, eventually forming a speckled mob. The *former students* were standing in the front rows. The tenants of basements and dank nooks were clustering at the door, grieved and worried. Women and men were all together. The truly miserable people rallied in the middle of the crowd: former decent people, who once had a social status but due to some misfortunes or excessive drinking, ended up living in the asylum.

Prascovia, Erioma's wife, was standing behind everyone, in the back. Erioma himself was waiting up in the bell tower, happy to be useful and ready to greet the Archbishop with the sincerest ding-dongs. Fedotici was fretting around Father Gherasim.

There was an orderly excitement reigning inside the church, created by the high energy of the public who, taken out from its usual environment, was now feeling more lively,

150

especially since the situation was exceptional and solemn.

And behold! Clumsy and bashful, the first bells— the small ones, could be heard, followed by the louder and more confident middle ones and, in the end, by the low-pitched tone of the big bell. A cheerful clang filled the air.

The Archbishop appeared in the church doorway. The crowd fluttered. Vladika stepped towards the pulpit. He was wearing an old, worn-out cassock, squeezing his hat in his left hand. In his right hand, instead of the bishop's staff, he had a simple crutch. After praying in front of the iconostasis, he turned to the crowd and, leaning on his crutch, addressed everybody, speaking in a low voice:

"Glad to see you, brothers!"

The first rows were confused, not knowing if they should answer the Archbishop or not. The ones in the back tensely raised their heads.

"You are my children," continued Vladika. "You have been offered to me by our Lord Jesus Christ and I will answer for you before Him, at Judgment Day. What will I tell Him if I do not know you nor your life? This is why I have come here today: I want to know more about you and your life so that I can serve you to the best of my abilities. Whether you will listen to me or not, it's your choice. If you choose not to listen to me, I am no longer responsible for your actions. You will answer on your own. Now tell me, how do you live? Is your life any good? Are you satisfied with it?"

Vladika kept silent, waiting for the answer. Someone involuntarily sighed hard. One of the *former students* coughed in his fist and, after striving to take a posture as decent as he could, said:

"Life is bad, Your Grace!"

"What life? It can't be worse than this!" added another one.

The rows were fussing again. There were whines, coughs and, finally, distinct voices:

"This isn't life, but pure suffering!"

"Even convicts live better than we do!"

The women started whining here and there. A shaggy head rose from the crowd, covering everyone with his strong, brutal voice:

"You can see for yourself how our life is... Why then, are you still asking?"

"I can see," Vladika sighed. "And I don't think there is a life worse than yours. The problem is that the one living such a life often fails to acknowledge that he could change it for a better one. Even now, when you admit your life is sad and miserable, do you truly understand how awful it is? For many of you, life is ugly sometimes because you don't have proper clothes, you don't have enough food, no warm corner to sleep in, no money; but it is sufficient for these things to appear in your life to suddenly make it better. I say your life is awful because it leads you to death. Day by day, hour by hour, you die, the same way a tree, without rain and sunlight, dies. Let me give you an example."

Vladika pointed to an inmate from the asylum.

"Well, how is he? No signs of blood. The skin is not pale anymore but greenish-yellow. The eyes are sunk into the back of his head, his belly hangs from his body, his hands are shaky, his height—

no more than one and a half arsin[22]. How long will he live, I wonder? And if right now he receives a brand-new house, enough food and as much money as he wants, will he feel happy? No! I'm speaking from my own experience. Nevertheless, *he* is not the only one who complains about how harsh life is and who, in the end, dies. Often times, even the wealthy, the educated, the noble people curse their lives for they too will die. But the difference between him and them is that the latter will die like flowers in an orangery, while he will die like grass in the field. This is why not only your life is sad, but many others' as well. Am I speaking the truth?"

"Yes... the truth... the truth..." sighed the crowd, gathering closer and surrounding the Archbishop.

"And what are you going to do about it? Are you going to continue living like this? This is not life, but agony. Hunger and cold are bearable, but can you still endure the hatred look of the world? You wander around the town like outsiders. Nobody smiles at you. The kindest hurry to toss you a coin, only to be left alone quicker. You cannot even conceive that a townsman would greet and invite you for a tea. People have distanced themselves from you. They care more about their animals than about you. Even dogs have a collar in case they get lost. But if you lose your way, nobody would bother at all. You are outlaws! Do you realize that...?"

Vladika was speaking slowly, heavily breathing and emphasizing each word. The words were heavy, falling like lead on their souls.

153

---

22 Arsin – Old Russian unit of measurement equal to 2.33 feet.

The crowd kept silent.

Vladika was silent too. He grabbed his staff with both hands, lowered his head down, fixing his eyes on the floor and pondered sorrowfully.

The others lowered their forehead down as well. A heavy silence covered the church. Each of them was thinking now about their own grief.

"I did not come here to hit the nail on the head," said Vladika in a loud voice, raising his forehead. "I've come here to tell you that there is another life which leads you not to your death, but to eternal life. I've come to tell you that you too can experience this life and, if you follow my words and live the way I'll teach you, then *you*"— he pointed to the same student — "will change from greenish yellow to rosy, from helpless to strong, from ill to healthy, from pitiable to smart, and all the other things will naturally follow afterward: the house, the food, etc. For a smart and healthy man will always manage to overcome any burden. And all of you who today are deplorable, wretched and useless, will become free people, citizens with full rights, and brothers to everybody, and every man shall want to be your friend. More than that, you will be liberated from all diseases and sufferings that even money cannot heal. And that is not all. So listen up all of you who have ears to listen!"

Vladika's voice was already echoing like thunder.

"Listen to what awaits you if you choose to live the way I teach you: every day you shall feel that your path goes not to destruction but to eternal life, for each of you shall realize death cannot defeat you. Death will seem impossible. And

154

when the days of your old age approach, you shall lean down, like a ripe wheat ear on damp soil. You will fall asleep without suffering, without fear, but cheerful and happy. Even if you are to be buried, you will not die, for you will be alive; you'll leave your body and, even if you are invisible to us, you will still see and hear yourselves. You will be alive! Do you want such life? Can you dare to believe in it? Can you believe it is obtainable by the power of our Lord Jesus Christ, who was the first to live this life on earth and taught it to the people, giving them the powers to obtain it? I ask you: can you believe that anything you ask of God you shall be given? CAN YOU?!"

Vladika's voice broke. His last word shook the entire church. After that, everything was silent... In the back, something heavy had dropped. A heartbreaking scream, followed by a thump of feet on the floor– probably someone had fallen and was now writhing on the floor.

"Oh no... NO... Oh, God... No... NO...!"

Taken by surprise, the terrified mob rushed forward towards the pulpit, and only the authoritative voice of the Archbishop made it stop:

"STOP! What happened?"

The commanding tone of the Archbishop had an immediate effect. The crowd stopped and calmed down in a blink of an eye. Someone next to Vladika said:

"A klikuska[23], probably..."

"It's a woman... she's sick... The wife of the church keeper... She has attacks..." explained Father Gherasim.

---

23 Klikuska – Generic name for possessed, demonized women.

The space around the possessed woman was cleared instantly. The poor lady continued to scream and writhe. Bewildered, Erioma was revolving around her, not knowing what to do.

"Bring her to me," said Vladika.

A few stronger men from the ones standing next to the klikuska grabbed her armpits and brought her in front of the pulpit.

"Give me some Holy Water," Vladika asked Father Gherasim.

"In the Name of the Father, and of the Son, and of the Holy Spirit!"

Vladika blessed her and abundantly sprinkled her three times with Holy Water.

"Calm down, my daughter! Stand up!"

Praskovia obeyed painstakingly. She stood up and leaned in front of the Archbishop. The Holy Water was pouring down her face.

"Wipe your face, child!" ordered Vladika.

Father Gherasim quickly brought a towel from the altar.

"Your soul has been filled with pain. You suffer too much... Come here. Tell me, what troubles you?" Vladika said gently and, retreating to the lectern, he stopped by the analogion[24].

With broken steps, barely dragging her feet, Praskovia approached the Archbishop.

"Brothers, move a little farther," he ordered the people.

The mob withdrew with a mysterious thrill, curiously looking at the Archbishop. He was

---

24 Analogion – A lectern or slanted stand on which icons or the Gospel are placed for veneration by the faithful in the Orthodox Church. It may also be used to read from liturgical books during the divine services.

leaning above the analogion. Praskovia whispered to him something, whining from time to time.

After a few minutes, Erioma was called to the analogion.

A quarter of an hour had passed. The crowd could only hear the murmur of whispers exchanged between Vladika, Erioma, and Paskovia. The words themselves were indiscernible. After a while, Vladika straightened his back and told them in a loud voice:

"Go in peace and do what I've told you. If you follow my words, your wish will be fulfilled too..."

Erioma stepped down from the pulpit with his face all red and big drops of sweat on his forehead. Praskovia was stepping calmly; her face had been lightened up with an unexpected joy. Something happened, and it seemed it was something good. The crowd felt it and surrounded the Archbishop who had already returned to his place, in a tight circle.

157

"I was telling you that by the power of our Lord Jesus Christ, man can receive whatever he desires. These two have asked for something and it will be given to them, and all of you shall stand as witnesses. But they will only receive it if they choose the life I am calling you to live. Listen to me! Take on this life's path while you still haven't perished. I do not ask much. For starters, I only ask you to unite in a community and listen to what the leaders, who are about to be appointed, will tell you. Will you do that?"

"Yes, we will! Yes, we will!"

"Will you agree?"

"We'll agree!"

"Well then, organize yourselves into a single society and a single parish. Father Gherasim and Father Paul will tell you how it is possible to pass from your old life to the new one, as they are the shepherds I'm giving you. They will lead you. But they need a helping hand. You will choose it from amongst you, right now! Whom do you wish to choose?"

The mob started whispering invigorated. Not long after, the voices were clear:

"Ataman! Ataman! Iaska the Ataman!"

Iaska the Ataman was known in the entire town. He was a clever and rangy vagabond, whose hideouts had long been searched by the police, but thanks to his ideal ability to come clean out of every situation, he managed to escape every time. Iaska was also different due to his extraordinary organizational skills that made him the leader of several gangs of rascals. The inmates from the asylum were afraid of the Ataman and had respect for him. They voted for him in this case too, since they were used to always see him as a leader.

However, a short old man, probably a former peasant, after squeezing himself through the crowd until he reached Vladika, stepped forward and said harshly:

"Iaska is not good... no... This is a different matter. A holy matter. Hmm... The Ataman is a master of dirty jobs. He's not right for it. No... We need another..."

"We don't need the Ataman; we don't need him!" the crowd shouted this time.

The voices were divided, creating a dispute. Its subject, Iaska the Ataman, was standing in a corner, leaning against the wall with his arms crossed over his chest. He was observing the crowd from beneath his eyebrows, heavyhearted.

Vladika kept silent, attentively looking at the Ataman. After a while, he decided to end to the dispute, explaining to the people that a man's previous life should not be taken into account, and gave Apostle Paul as an example who, initially, persecuted Christ after which he became a zealous minister of His. Vladika's words seemed to have worked upon Iaska, for the vagabond stepped in front of the crowd to personally withdraw his nomination.

"I'm not right," he admitted.

"If you would have said you were,"— Vladika responded— "it would have meant you didn't change at all. But since you reflected on your deeds and refused, you proved that you understand what kind of task this is. Start today. The first thing you have to do is not allow anyone in the streets today. The church will give you money for food,"— Vladika gave money to Father Gherasim— "Send two-three men to buy food and bring it back here. You will eat in the church too, after which Father Gherasim will explain to you the next steps. But now let us pray to God to give us His blessing for a good start."

Vladika blessed Father Gherasim to start the *Te-Deum Service*, then joined the crowd and started singing in a loud voice:

"Heavenly Father..."

The crowd took over the solemn melody of the prayer but not without showing a bit of clumsiness and, one by one, they started to kneel.

"Vladika," asked Father Gherasim, while seeing the Archbishop to the door. "How did you manage to calm Praskovia and make her believe so firmly in the fulfillment of her wish? I've had many similar cases during my life, but I've always been helpless..."

"Fasting and praying are recommended to the married couple in such cases, so they can receive Communion with the Holy Sacraments. This type of demons can only be driven out with fasting and praying. This is why they are so important..."

Vladika leaned closer to the Father's ear and spoke with him for about ten minutes.

"Remember to always give such remedies to such couples," Vladika ended his words. "And tie this sin. You can untie it in different circumstances. It will very much depend upon your perspicacity. Well, go now, finish your discussion..."

160

Father Gherasim returned to the church, amazed of the profoundness with which Vladika could understand the human nature; a profoundness that the Archbishop proved when he explained some subtleties regarding the Sacrament of Confession.

XIV

I n town, the days carried on cheerfully. Summer theaters and winter ballets, clubs, gatherings, restaurants, public gardens— there was a bit of everything for the citizens to fully enjoy life and spend their free time in careless delight. And the citizens took full advantage of it. Music was always playing in parks, and plays were always performed in the theatres. Purebred trotters could be seen flying up and down the town streets from dawn to dusk. The sidewalks were filled with townspeople, walking and showing off the elegance of their clothes.

161

The euphoria of the people ready to have fun would often be ruined by one thing. Whenever they would go out for a walk determined to spend the afternoon hours as joyful as possible after a copious meal, they would stumble across a dry hand, often with its fingers cut and accompanied by the same false and sad cry: "Have mercy, in the name of Christ." And if the citizen in cause would show his kindness and tossed him a coin, he would get into a bigger trouble; other ten beggars, from all over the street corners, would swoop on him, snatching a piece or two for themselves.

All these beggars, paupers, vagabonds, real or fake cripples, and all kinds of petty pilferers and cheeky hoodlums were more disturbing to the town residents than mosquitos or flies. In vain did all sorts of committees, societies, and settlements fight against this blight. In vain did the police struggled with it: despite all the measures taken against beggary, the number of beggars increased with each day, becoming more and more annoying.

Yet, today was the day when the townspeople noticed that this unpleasant and aggressive element had suddenly and almost completely disappeared. The streets were empty as if somebody had used a magic wand to make the beggars disappear. Their absence was so striking that everybody had noticed it. So the townspeople, accustomed to having great difficulties in getting rid of the beggars, were now wondering where did they all vanish. Some of the citizens, more curious than others, went looking for the vagabonds.

They found all of them at the Archbishop's villa.

The ones who found them were perplexed by their discovery; about five hundred people: men, women, and children of different ages were swarming on a large patch of land that opened towards the villa. Many were digging gutters, some were carrying building materials, while others had already started building an entire row of houses.

There was something extraordinary about this scenery.

In town, the rumors of vagabonds building houses for themselves spread rapidly. In the meantime, the works were advancing at a fast pacing. Father Gherasim was working tirelessly on arranging his new parish conceived by the bishop. The most difficult thing for him was maintaining the enthusiasm stirred by the Archbishop in the *asylum inmates*. But his oratorical talent proved to be very helpful. His words worked miracles on the crowd since now they were not just beautiful and empty words. Everybody had a meaningful and definite goal now. Everybody felt the earth under their feet, pursuing the path that led them to their objective. They were walking on, however, feeling tired nevertheless. In such moments, the best remedy was Father Gherasim's refreshing words of encouragement.

While Father Gherasim spirited the people with his words, Father Paul was in charge of the hoe and the hammer. His gigantic pose kept appearing everywhere, carefully observing the worksite. Whenever he would notice a decline in the workers' pace, he would rush and help, bringing the hammer, crowbar or his shovel. The tramping of the weak workers, encouraged by Father Paul, would immediately be sprightly heard.

163

However, not all of them were able to savor in the general enthusiasm. For some, words and examples were not convincing enough. They would even dare to cause troubles. This was the part where The Ataman would intervene. He would grumpily approach the brawler, threateningly put his muscular arm on his shoulder, and would pierce him with his big, black eyes. Sometimes, this gesture alone was sufficient to solve the situation, since everybody knew that The Ataman didn't like to joke.

Along with the works in the hamlet, a similar dynamic activity was taking place in town. A group of priests led by Father Grigori was looking for possibilities to finance the constructions. The church offertories were stacked up penny by penny, gathering the necessary money through spirited sermons and ardent phone calls. The final sum was then paid as a loan with no interest to the Novoduhovsk[25] parish, as the hamlet was named.

Vladika had visited the site about five times. All works would stop at his arrival and everybody would rush to greet him. The Archbishop would sit on a log or a rock and would start talking. Half an hour later, when Vladika would leave, everybody would resume their work with more diligence.

The land destined for the hamlet was divided into plots; each plot was meant to be settled by one family. A house was built separately, for each family. In time, both the house and the land would become the property of the tenants. But for the moment, everything was to be done in common: they were working and designing the houses' blueprints together, according to their skills.

The works would begin every day at the sound of the bells, but not before the mob, together with the Fathers, had sung a prayer outside under the clear sky. At nights, the workers would find shelter and sleep at the villa. Father

164

25 Novoduhovsk – New Spirit (*Literal Translation*).

Gherasim would rush into town to speak with the Archbishop, almost every time at the end of a working day. Vladika would greet him with the same words:

"Well, how are the things going?"

The report would begin:

"They are working perseveringly; the enthusiasm is not fading. Mitiuhin and Kudreas quit drinking... Vaniuha still runs away at nights but returns in the morning eventually. Akseniha stopped coughing. Nikiticina had surgery. Mitiuha overcame nostalgia and started working."

"Praised be the Lord!" Vladika would answer gladly.

"We have many new people, Your Grace," continued Father Gherasim. "What should we do with them? They are coming from all of the surrounding villages, asking to be accepted into our parish. To refuse them– one cannot, out of pity; to take them in– neither the land nor the money is sufficient..."

"Don't refuse anybody! But make sure they are accepted by the whole community, not only by you. We'll acquire more land. As for the financial means, no need to worry. First of all, the state treasury is required to give us a subsidy because, by having brought these wretches back to life, the state gained future taxpayers and citizens with juridical capacity. Secondly, there are no vagabonds left in town, therefore, all the philanthropic institutions that once swarmed around your parishioners will now transfer the money to us. For clearing the town of the *disruptive elements*, we will oblige the local administration to give us more funds. Later, we can call on the

165

wealthy Christians to fulfill their duty of loving their neighbor. Nothing will stand in my way!

"If they won't give us gold and silver from their own pockets, I'll bless the clergy to take it from the altar. The day before Pascha, I will lock up all the churches and bell towers, keeping them closed until Christians will fulfill their first and most important commandment. Believe me, the silence of the church bells on the day of Pascha in our holy Russia will shiver even the heart of the most callous atheist man that ever lived, for it will be more dreadful than the lugubrious quietness of the graves, and more terrifying than the sinister silence before the storm.

"However, I don't think my parishioners will determine me to go that far. The Russian people are merciful by nature. There are wealthy people, yes, but never will Russia give birth to individuals like Rothschild. It hasn't become so foul, still... But I haven't called out the people for sacrifices yet. For years, we have been teaching them to donate money for our vestments, bells, oil, incense, the candles and food for the ascetics... We only prompted people towards true charity. If we steer this quality of the Russian people in the right direction, we'll witness pure miracles taking place, despite the reasoning and the course of political and economic laws of the West. But before the people will start to object, take from my salary."

"It has been taken for this month, Your Grace," answered Father Gherasim, revealing a sincere respect for the generous Archbishop.

"Then take the next one in advance... How is Father Paul?"

"He's working tirelessly…"

"Has he brought his family here yet?"

"No. He's too busy working"

"Tell him to go and bring them here." Even his cassock is completely ripped, Vladika would think to himself about Father Gherasim until, one day, the hierarch rummaged his wardrobe and gave Father Gherasim one of his own cassocks.

Father Gherasim's reports were not always encouraging. Sometimes, the Father would worry about the success of the *enterprise* because of the slow pace with which the works were advancing. Since the people were still weak and there weren't any real craftsmen among them, the Father asked whether they could pay for the services of real contractors.

"No, no, God forbid! Each pebble, each stick must be placed with their own hands otherwise they'll care about these buildings no more than they used to care about the asylums and the shelter houses of the town. Man values only what he makes with his own hands. What is easily received and with no labor cannot be cherished. Do not let the aesthetic side of the constructions worry you. Even a handicap baby receives love from his parents. Anything else?"

"Afanasici and Kudlatii wish to go back to their old vagrant life."

The Archbishop takes thoughts, worried, after which he repeated again what he heard:

"Afanasici and Kudlatii are giving up, you say?"

"Yes, Your Grace. I fear others more may follow."

167

"And what did they say, more precisely? Did they mention what draws them back?"

"They didn't say anything directly. I conclude it myself because they grow lazier with each passing day."

"This may also be a consequence of their lack of good habits. They've lost the practice of working since they became vagabonds. The works are probably too much for them, I suppose. It is risky. Only the work executed within one's working limits can be healing. Do not let them nor anyone else overwork themselves. And one more thing. There is a spring with fresh, cold water near the villa. Dig a hole just below the spring of water, bless the water and have them drink it and submerge in the water daily. This will strengthen their body and cast away their laziness. In the end, laziness is but a disease. You can tell almost all of them to do it. From what I've noticed, with a few exceptions, nobody has a shattered health. I think we should give them some extra time for resting apart from Sundays. By the way, there will be two holidays soon: Saturday and Sunday. Stop working on Thursday afternoon and let them wash, clean, take a bath. Tell them to fast on Friday and Saturday, and have them receive Communion with the Holy Gifts on Sunday. There should be such fasting more often. At first, once a month. On holy days, pray together all the way from the church to the working site. In the evenings, continue to have discussions and readings, and don't follow any lecture schedule, just speak from your heart."

Father Gherasim would strictly follow the recommendations of the Archbishop and would return to him, asking for more. Life was boiling and although the things that happened every day were understood by the Father, for greater security, he preferred to ask Vladika for advice.

XV

pring came. The days offered everything that would please a man during this season: the warm sun, the birds chirping, the clear bright blue of the sky. More splendid than ever, the Volga was calmly waving the ships that were sailing on their usual routes. On one of these vessels, Father Paul was carrying his family to his new workplace.

The Father's wife, who was traveling such a long distance by ship for the first time, was sitting on the deck, contemplating at the wonderful scenery. Their four children were playing around. Father Paul was walking back and forth, glowing of happiness and vitality.

"I look at you and I can't stop wondering," said his wife. "I don't understand what makes you so happy. Only Lord knows what kind of parish you have received! A hamlet of vagabonds and two priests! Will we at least make enough for food? Oh, Pavlusha... In vain did you bristle then. What would have cost you if you had gone to the monastery, enduring a little austerity, until your canon would have completed? We'd be living back at our old place in peace by now. It was a good parish after all..."

"Nothing of the kind! We don't know that! Have you thought that I could have become a drunkard at the monastery? Would you have preferred living your life, even though sufficient and with no shortages, with an alcoholic husband? The responsibilities of this job will be different. Sometimes you would be ready to starve all your life, sacrificing yourself for the job, for the job itself represents a source of happiness and gives the man so much fulfillment that not even all Rothschild's money can buy."

"Well, aren't you going to be a priest there too? You will still minister the Vespers and Liturgies, baptize and bury, read sermons... and, maybe, you'll also teach the children at school..."

"Yes and no," the Father said contemplatively, sitting on the little bench next to his wife. "Do you remember our neighbor, Mary-the alewife, who wanted to learn from you the skill of taking care of the household? She did everything you did; she fed the animals, cooked broth, laid the bed. But did she have the same results as you? Our cow gave us almost two buckets of milk, while hers barely two jugs, even if the cows were of the same breed. In summer, you filled the courtyard with baby chickens, and our cellar was full of smoked meat goodies. But all her baby chicks died in spring..."

"Well, it's not so difficult to understand, Pavlusha. Even though she tried to do things exactly as I did, she didn't do them properly. She might have prepared the cow's hogwash using my recipe, but she didn't serve it on time or had missed something else along the way, and that's why the results were different..."

"And isn't it the same with us as well? You say that I'm still going to be a priest in the new parish, and you're correct. But this time, I'll be an actual priest! Do you know how I was before? Like our neighbor. On one side, she thought she did everything correctly, but in reality, she either didn't do it on time or she did something else instead. Imagine a healthy newborn boy. At seventeen years, he'll be a strong fellow, his blood pumping like a whirligig through his veins. Perfect for marriage. But will we believe that? No. We'll assume it's not the time, so we'll have him wait a bit longer. In papers, he's still underage. But until he'll be of legal age on papers, the lad will become barren, wasting his strength Lord knows where! On the other hand, a man, not even in his thirties, is considered to be ideal for marriage even though he had already squandered his vigor. One such as him should first be sent to the monastery to learn abstinence and have his vitality restored. Only after that should he consider getting married. But the world order of things is upside down; we agree that he should get married whenever he wishes, for his papers are in order and there isn't any legal impediment.

"Let's take another example. The man falls sick in bed, he's upset... One such as him should be brought to Confession. He should Confess properly, have all his problems fixed, be brought to the righteous path and, in the end, receive Communion. But in reality, nobody even looks at him because nobody considers him a priority.

And if it happens for him to come to Confession on his own initiative, the priest bluntly tells him: 'Are you crazy, man? Wait for the Great Fasting and I'll give you Communion then.' And so, in the first case, the faithful slips the priest's mind and, in the latter, the priest doesn't attend him on time. The result is that, although we baptize, marry, hear their confession and give them Communion, people remain like they were before... Should we do it knowingly and skillfully, the result would completely be different."

"You should have attended that course at the Academy, Pavlusha, and you would have learned about these things earlier. Looks like the seminary didn't really teach you all of it..."

"No, Masha[26]! Neither the seminary nor the Academy has anything to do with this. This awareness cannot be achieved by studying. In town, I saw priest-academics, academic-priests, magistrates, even doctors in theology. It's frightening to see so many educated people out there! But neither of them manages to do everything accordingly. On the contrary, they do even less than us, rural priests. At least, our parishioners still come to church, unlike theirs."

"They preach too little, not teaching the people properly."

I doubt it... they teach, preach, provide lectures, catechize, hold conferences. Some of them preach quite well, actually. From time to time, one would come out to the pulpit and preach so emotional that his words would make your eyes water. And if we, the priests, are not accustomed to sermons, then who is? It touches

---

26 Masha – Diminutive name for Maria.

your heart sometimes. But still, it continues to remain senseless. Words are nothing more than mere words. After all, how could it be different? Words must be in alignment with one's soul for them to have a meaning. But do you think we are able to do that? Decide for yourself. For example, take Anempodist Fiodorovici, the chief of the village's train station. He used to come to our church. It so happened that he attended the sermon right when I was preaching about generosity and love for our neighbor. So after I finished my preaching, I sent the churchwarden with the tray to him, asking for money to help the church. So much grief I felt when he threw only grivna[27]. 'Look at him, the skinflint!' I thought. But then again, I quickly realized that he couldn't give more than two grivna. His wage was about eighty rubles. Because Anempodist Fiodorovici was anemic and had cataracts, from his paycheck, forty rubles would be spent for food. It's possible to buy food with just ten rubles, of course, if you want to eat only borscht and kasha. However, with such food, Anempodist would have left this world in less than half a year. Therefore, to live well, he required a chef, healthy food, and vodka with soda. His wife was sick too and couldn't manage to look after the children nor the household by herself, so, willingly or not, they hired a nanny. The same goes with clothing– he couldn't dress with whatever he could find because, by being so fragile and lacking a proper coat, he would immediately catch a cold.

175

---

27 Grivna – Currency unit, currently the national currency of Ukraine.

"Then there's the doctor, the midwife, and at least one newspaper per day– still needed to be paid, right? And now, tell me: is he left with anything at all? He is forced to budget every nickel, not just a two-grivna coin. But alas, there's more to it: could Anempodist Fiodorovici be asked to show generosity and make sacrifices for the benefit of his neighbor? In other words, is it reasonable to tell him to live on borscht and kasha, and give the money saved on food and clothes to a hungry person? This would mean to send him straight to death. And for what? To give another man the possibility to live? It's absurd to let someone die so that another can live..."

"You, Pavlusha, have completely changed and started to think somehow different since you left for the new eparchy... I don't quite understand you anymore..."

"And you won't understand until you too will change your opinion about people. Do you remember what we used to think about our neighbors, the boyars? Remember how many people would visit their residence? Coachmen, chefs, footmen, chambermaids, tutors, nannies, governors... but where did they live during the year? In winter – in the town and in summer – in Pyatigorsk or abroad, in Karlsbad... We felt outraged, thinking that these boyars needed all the pleasure of life just to have fun. How come these people couldn't see anything sinful in such pleasures when others around them were dying of starvation?!

"In fact, our boyars need all those things to sustain their lives and if we take them away, they would all disappear. The same goes for our peasants. If they wouldn't have what to eat, they would all perish..."

"Well, now you're beating around the bush," his wife smiled. "From what you are saying, fancy hats and theatres are also indispensable for their life?"

"How else then? Take away the hat from the lady and, along with it, you take away the entire essence of her life. Maybe, she's practicing her mental activity by inventing new fancy hats; if you would deprive her of this, her mind would run out of work. Theatres as well; close down all these theatres, clubs, restaurants, etc., and our noblemen would hang themselves in sorrow. Or when winter comes, if they could not find a job, our peasants would turn to drinking..."

"I can't agree with you. There is something in your words that puzzles me... Does it mean you are finding pretexts for those who use the comforting of life to their benefit, while others are starving?"

"I didn't say anything about whether I think they're justified to live such life or not. I've only explained that Anempodist Fiodorovici cannot live without a chef, a nanny, brandy, soda and further on— without a tutor, without Pyatigorsk, without a pension, etc. For him, all these things are not a luxury but an acute necessity. I said this to highlight the fact that one cannot ask Anempodist Fiodorovici to serve his neighbor, not even in the form of two grivna. And I'll also add that he cannot even be asked to self-improve. For a man to improve, a series of circumstances is necessary. Usually, a man educates himself by reading books. The ascetics of the desert did it using deep meditation. Can Anempodist Fiodorovici read or deeply meditate? Hypothetically speaking, yes, he can. In reality, he cannot. Why? He wakes up in the morning and goes to work. He is there until three or four. He comes home, has lunch and automatically becomes incapable of doing any other work. To be fit for the next day, he needs rest, silence, healthy diet, fresh air... When can he read or meditate? Plus, it's possible that Anempodist Fiodorovici loses his thinking ability with the passing of time. So when a priest asks him to serve his neighbor and to perfect himself, he's actually asking him to do the impossible. Because of this, our preaching is hollow. And all of us, both the ones who teach others and the ones who learn on their own, are becoming more and more like Anempodist Fiodorovici's..."

"But then what are we supposed to do with the hungry?"

"With the hungry...? Some say: 'Away with people like Anempodist Fiodorovici, they cost us too much. Let them die and instead, we'll have people who eat only borscht and kasha and can still perform like him. Then there'll be leftovers for the hungry too. What do you think, is this wise?"

"It seems to be logical, it's just that..."

"Just what?"

"Something doesn't add up... But I can't seem to figure out what."

"Let me enlighten you then. The thing is that nothing will be left for the hungry even if other people would replace the *anempodists*. They cannot live long only with kasha and borscht. With an inevitable fatalism, slowly, they too will reach the same condition like Anempodist Fiodorovici. Everything in this world grows old, wears out and maintaining something old is more expensive than buying something new. A man grows old not only individually but within a generation as well, so to speak. Worn-out people give birth to a weaker generation which, in turn, gives birth to a completely helpless one. The life of this last generation will become more expensive, for the same reason the life of a sick man is costlier than the life of a healthier one. Only inside a beehive is a bee different than a bumblebee. The beekeeper only acts rationally when he kills a part of the bumblebees to keep the honey. The same cannot be done with people, even though, in time, all men become like bumblebees. But until this truth is obvious for everyone, the man in question will continue to procreate freely, giving birth to heirs who become, hard to differentiate from the start, either working bees or bumblebees. If you start killing bumblebees, then, in no time, there will be no trace of humanity left."

"So then what can be done?"

"Well, the main purpose of our ministry is the renewal of man; from an always sick and grumpy individual, capable of little effort, like Anempodist Fiodorovici, to a healthy, working, vigorous and lively person, who spends eight or nine hours at work without getting tired and still is able to spend another seven to eight hours working on himself, eating healthy, without the need of plum brandy, soda, or Lord knows what diets, and being satisfied with only borscht and

179

kasha. Then, the food will be enough for the hungry as well. It will be enough for everybody."

"Don't you have to be a doctor to do that?"

"Where necessary, we must be doctors too... In the Old Testament, among all other things, priests were also doctors. Nowadays, a priest doesn't need to be a doctor because there are professionals, but it's absolutely necessary for him to know exactly when to send a man to the doctor or when to call him for Confession. And no matter if with medicine or prayer, with the surgeon's scalpel or with the preaching, the priest must free the man from this avalanche of shortages in which he is suffocating – first liberating his soul, of course – so that afterwards, by giving him mobility, he can be led on the path with no end of which Jesus spoke about two thousand years ago: *You, therefore, must be perfect, as your heavenly Father is perfect...*"

"I thought that your only responsibility was praying to God and redeeming souls..." said the woman meditating.

"Redeeming souls...?!" repeated the Father, bursting into a joyful laughter.

"What is it?"

"Nothing... I've just remembered my years at the seminary. We used to gather and argue with each other: 'Prove this man has a soul...'"

"And what's so funny about that?"

"Not at all funny, indeed, but upsetting. People have created for themselves some sort of a theological *soul* and they're struggling to prove its existence. Obviously, they'll never prove anything..."

"You're talking nonsense again. Didn't God create the soul?"

"Yes, God did create the soul except people have totally forgotten about the soul He created and so they created their own *soul*. Vladika spoke very well about it. Once, Father Gherasim and I visited him. We started talking... He spoke clearly and meaningfully and always showed how things were. I'm not sure if I can explain them to you in the same way..."

The Father stopped for a while, meditated about something and said:

"What do you think? Is there a rooster inside an egg?"

"What do you mean...? What's with this stupid question?"

"Well, you see, the question of the soul within the man is as dull as this one. There is no rooster inside an egg, of course, but in some situations, a baby chick can hatch from an egg and can grow into a rooster. Man is an egg too and, as long as he remains an egg, he can hardly be distinguished from other creatures. He needs special circumstances for his soul to develop within and transform him into a human being with free will. This profound being must first be strengthened in spirit, so he can shed away the coat of the flesh like an eggshell, and then come to God, the One who will perfect him. This is what *redeeming people* means."

The woman sank into her thoughts, trying to grasp these new ideas her husband was telling her.

"It's overwhelming when you think of the huge responsibility that priests carry!" the Father

181

continued. "How will you call the mother who prematurely gives birth, even if out of ignorance, to her children that, later on, perceive themselves as unprepared for life? These children will feel that a great part of their torments is due to their parents who precipitately brought them into this world, and start condemning them. Instinctively, Christians too feel that their spiritual fathers, priests who renew them through the Holy Baptism, sent them unprepared into the other world. This is why they are fretting, blaming and calling them 'priests with long manes'..."

The woman was still thinking. Lately, she has had many surprises: the journey, Father Paul's new ideas, Father Paul himself, who returned completely transformed after their long separation... All these things aroused various thoughts in her head, thoughts that she was hurrying to put in order.

The Father went looking for the children who got lost somewhere on the deck.

"And is this possible?" she asked him when he returned.

"What?"

"To do as you said... to transform men into spirits..."

"For a human, it is impossible. This is the reason why the Son of God had to descend into the world. Christ gave men a new power amongst the others that were working in this world, and since then, it started to be possible. This is the very power with which priests and bishops work..."

"Is there such a power inside you too?" asked the woman refreshing herself, looking curiously and with admiration at Father Paul.

"The priests have it," answered the Father convinced. "But not everyone who wears a cassock is a priest. I am only ordained a priest. But now, I believe that the power of God is working in the world and that men can master it, and that is why, maybe, I'll become a priest myself... Had I peacefully remained at the old parish, I would have become an Anempodist Fiodorovici, I would have drunk brandy with soda, spending my summers at Pyatigorsk. But for maintaining that, I would have needed a lot of money; so I would have fought my parishioners for every penny during funerals and home blessings..."

Father Paul bowed his forehead, staring into the blue river. The water was bubbling under the strokes of the propellers, raising white, foamy waves. The waves were running and playing a merry game, shining in the warm sunshine, reflecting all the colors of the rainbow. The ship was sailing fast but the Father's thoughts were far ahead. In his mind, he could already see the quay and Father Gherasim, happily greeting him... First, they would all go to Vladika to ask for the blessing. There he was, Vladika, always kind, always thinking about his flock. He would warmly congratulate him on the occasion of their arrival and would bless his family.

And there it was, Novoduhovsk, at last. Everything was still in its beginning. The parishioners hurried to greet them. They were happy, kind, but... much work was still needed to transform them into God's thoughtful beings...

183

Many years of hard work were waiting for them ahead. But Lord, so easy and joyful this work was...

Father Paul didn't anticipate everything in his thoughts. It wasn't just Father Gherasim who was waiting for him on the quay. Next to the priest, nervous and somehow solemn, was Erioma. He was holding a big bouquet of wildflowers. When the guests stepped on the shore, Erioma received the blessings from Father Paul, solemnly approached the Father's wife, handed her the flowers, blushing and abashedly smiling, and asked her to accept the honor of becoming the godmother of his child.

"Did she...?" asked Father Paul amazed.

"Yesterday..." said Erioma smiling. "God gave me a daughter!"

The priests exchanged meaningful glances between them.

XVI

―――◆⬦◆―――

Why in such a hurry, doctor?" Father Vladimir asked Father Gherasim's old acquaintance, catching him in the street.

The doctor was hurrying, lost in his thought, when he was interrupted by the priest. Quickly shaking his hand, he mumbled, half embarrassed and half annoyed:

"To the missionary dispute!"

"Where?!" asked the Father surprised.

"To your debate with the Starovers[28]."

"What happened to you? From what I knew, you were not such a big fan of such things," said Father Vladimir smiling.

"A man learns as long as he lives!" the doctor avoided a direct answer.

Then he took out a cigarette and lit it.

"Since when have you long embraced such philosophies? I hardly noticed it about you before..."

---

28 Starover – Old faith believer. Orthodox of the old rite who refused to accept Patriarch Nikon's reforms imposed upon the Russian Orthodox Church. Recently, they were accepted back in the Church by the Moscow Patriarchate.

"So many things we never notice... We walk like ants under the moon, imagining we know everything."

"But, in fact, *I only know that I know nothing...*"

"Precisely... So difficult it is in one's old age to realize that one too got slapped by this Socratic hand, destined for human knowledge! While one's young, let him be...! It may even prove to be useful being troubled by such cursed questions. But after one escapes the sickness of the youth, one stops at a certain point and creates for himself a complete, exhaustive concept, living convinced that, from now on, everything will be crystal clear, having a *thank you* prepared for every *hello*. Well, at that precise moment, somebody comes and, bam! Makes one doubt his absolute equilibrium, and thus, everything goes down the drain..."

"And who did that to you?"

"This Vladika of yours..."

"Have you seen him? Have you spoken to him? Has he managed to convince you of the authenticity of Christianity?"

"Not convincing, per say, but he made me wonder, though."

"It's interesting how he acted upon your incurable skepticism towards all the sources of Christian theology..."

"In no way with quotes from the Scriptures!"

"With what then? Facts from science?"

"No, no... One cannot catch us off guard using that anymore. We know these theological arguments of *rational origin*. You build theological systems with all sorts of conclusions based on premises that cannot be verified and then, in order to consolidate them, you invoke facts offered by science: 'You know, science says it too...' But whatever science says apart from reason is silenced. No, there is something completely different about him. While talking to me, he did not even mention Christianity. He kept on speaking about doctors and medicine, but everything came out in such a way that one had to agree that healing people outside Christianity is like pouring water into a sieve..."

"Does Vladika know medicine?"

"I cannot say. He's got little practical knowledge but he reveals to you the philosophy of this science, so to say. Indeed..."— the doctor threw huffily the cigarette stump— "what does our work offer man? We heal, treat, cure, and people become weaker and weaker. Vladika proposes that we renew people, that we change the mentality of the retarded man, making him human again. I wanted to tell him that neither he nor anybody else can do this but then I remembered his hamlet of vagabonds, so I thought about it a little more. Whether you like it or not, Novoduhovsk obliges you to give credence to Vladika's words. The word sustained by facts is, yet, a great force. I've always been skeptical about such adventures, especially after the downfall of Tolstoyist colonies in which I too was active once. Well, in Vladika's case, facts speak for themselves. I hardly recognize the former *asylum inmates*... Do you know what an *asylum inmate* means? If we are to use the theological language, it's easier to move a mountain than to convince one of them to climb only a step in the stairway to perfection. And he's done it..."

187

"Over here, Pavel Ivanovici, over here, come!" shouted Father Vladimir at the sight of the professor approaching, interrupting the doctor. "We've taken everything. Let us proceed. By the way, it seems that His Grace is also taking part in the discussions."

"Don't count too much on your Vladika— the doctor restarted the conversation, visibly irritated by the interruption— he's not a specialist in raskols[29] after all. As far as I am concerned, I'd rather see these debates take place without archbishops. They are a little ignorant in such matters, and they like interfering. From time to time, one of them slips an inappropriate word, giving the missionary the difficult task of coming clean for both theology and the archbishop, as it happened with those conciliar vows, the most difficult points of missionarism defense. It would have been best if they had simply admitted from the start: 'Well, what can they do now, the hierarch has screwed up.' Instead, they rushed to cast anathema without properly understanding how things happened... No. You're better off carrying your disputes alone and strive not to involve Vladika. It's safer this way...

"Now then! The public has come in great number today. The debate will probably be a serious one..." concluded the doctor, looking satisfied at the crowd that kept rushing into the room.

Among the first comers, there was a group of people occupying a large corner of the hall. They

188

29 Raskol – Schism, faction. Raskolnikov is the name of the famous character in Dostoyevsky's novel, *Crime and Punishment*, and derives from the Russian *raskolnic*. The *raskolnic* is a divisive, revolting person.

were all dressed in the same way: shirts tied with belts, large trousers tucked in boots, and thick long coats fashioned from homemade fabric. They were calm, confident of their own dignity.

They were the representatives of Novoduhovsk. Two priests, wearing frocks of the same fabric as their parishioners' coats, were leading them. Father Paul, a lively and energetic man, was impatiently waiting for the opening of the debate, and to make time pass faster, he started talking to a parishioner or two.

Father Gherasim was waiting silently and calmly. The mark of his old tormented life had not been completely erased from his face. His forehead was wrinkled, his eyes glazed from under the same lowered eyebrows, but they were not the same exhausted, suffering, sad eyes from before. They were peaceful and serene, even bold, and reflected a bright light; they were eyes that had begun to see. His face betrayed an iron will. There were no signs left from his old hump. His back was straight; his chest was up. His sturdy arms, crossed on his chest, revealed a supplement of physical strength. Despite his gray hair, the Father looked young, healthy and full of energy. His young face expression and his gray locks formed an unusual contrast which attracted many stares. The ones who would pass by him would stop and bow respectfully.

In the hall, the bustle was increasing, but when the priests started to sing the prayer, the entire hall became silent.

"But aren't they going to wait for the Archbishop?" a gentleman asked his neighbor.

"The Archbishop is already there. Look…"

189

Having sneaked undetected through the crowd, Vladika was sitting on one of the chairs next to the great desk.

The silence filled the hall again.

The missionary approached the desk. The proposed subject for the debate was the lack of canonicity of the Austrian hierarchy. After talking a little about the necessity of the hierarchical Grace in the work of redeeming the faithful, the missionary plunged right into the subject. By making use of countless historical documents and references to ancient texts and strict logical deductions, and with the help of his natural oratorical talent, the missionary quickly attracted the public on his side. The missionary himself felt that too and began using more and more triumphant tones in his speech.

The conclusion of the discourse highlighted the lack of canonicity regarding the Austrian hierarchy, meaning the hierarchy lacked God's Grace and, therefore, all its followers were destined to ruin should they not adhere to the Orthodox Church.

The conclusion was found offensive by the Starovers (Old Believers) since it nominated them as certain candidates to hell. Also, equally offensive was the attitude of the Orthodox people who, fascinated by the missionary's speech, were throwing ironic looks at the Old Believers. Voices of protest could be heard from the Starovers, and so the dispute finally began.

Usually modest, the Starovers now had an egotistic, even provocative purpose, explained first of all, by their wish to not be humiliated in front of such a large audience, and secondly, by

The Manifesto of Tolerance, which was welcomed by many of them as a permission to speak their mind about the missionary openly and risk free.

The missionary successfully warded off the first attack from the Starovers and was now waiting for other replies. There were many who wanted to give them. The dispute flared up. The missionary completely forgot about the presence of the Archbishop who was silently listening to the speakers with no intention to take part in the discussion. The audience warmed up. The interest for the dispute grew, and exclamations of approval or disapproval could be heard from time to time. At times, the noise surpassed the limit of decency and the organizers had to call for silence.

Evidently weak at knowing the history of the Church and the dogmas of faith, the Starovers had their revenge by delivering clever answers and remarks and by using irony and sarcasm, often times too excessive, all addressed to the defenders of Orthodoxy. In this case, the one standing out the most was Afanasici Mitrici, famous among the Starovers for his quick-wittedness. His taunting observations sparked the laughter of the crowd every time.

Afanasici Mitrici was, as one could see, in his best shape. He was excited by the impressive number of the listeners as well as the presence of an Orthodox archbishop which, in the end, lead him over the line. Initially, Afanasici Mitrici was striving to demonstrate the fact that the Starovers held the Grace while the Orthodox hierarchy itself lacked it. Also, he wanted to prove that the antichrist had long been working within the Orthodox Church and that, therefore, all those who were obedient to it were servants of the devil, longed after by the fire of hell. Nobody from them would be saved. Only those of the Old Faith would go to heaven.

His words were fluent and well-rounded. His verbal attacks towards the missionary, sprinkled with jokes and jests, impressed the public. Afanasici Mitrici, however, didn't consider them to be enough. Encouraged by the approving glances of his followers, he decided to manifest himself in his entire splendor and to give his opponents the final blow. Having considered that the missionary was too insignificant as a target for his irony, he aimed all his cleverness towards the Orthodox bishops and then, switching from general to specific, he spoke of the Archbishop present in the hall.

192

The Starovers were smiling approvingly. The Orthodox were revolted. The air in the hall smelt like scandal. It was not long in coming.

In the paroxysm of eloquence, Afanasici Mitrici pointed his finger at the Archbishop and shouted:

"There he is... Behold, the antichrist! Follow him. He'll lead you on the path straight to Satan's den..."

Even the Starovers felt ashamed by such impertinence coming from their defender. The ones sitting next to Afanasici Mitrici grabbed him by his sleeves and forced him to sit down. The missionary, who did not have the inspiration to end this discussion, kept quiet and confused.

An awkward silence filled the room. All eyes were worryingly staring at Vladika.

XVII

fanasici Mitrici's rude outburst didn't impress the Archbishop at all. The hierarch slowly stood up, grabbed his staff and approached the desk in his usual majestic and imposing walk.

The entire hall was breathlessly waiting.

"Beloved brothers," the Archbishop began calmly, addressing everybody present. "Two carpenters were walking down a road, arguing about who was the best carpenter. The first one claimed he was the best, for only he possessed the true knowledge of the woodwork, while the rest of the carpenters were inferior to him. The second one called his comrade a liar, stating that he didn't know anything, then bragged about he, himself, as being the best carpenter. Their feud would never end... Brothers, how do you believe this quarrel should end? How can they agree on who is the best carpenter? In my opinion, they both should be given a task then we would see who is the best one. Perhaps, both of them would turn out to be equally good.

"Brothers, are we not like the two quarrelsome carpenters? We try to prove to each other whose hierarchy truly possesses God's Grace, the heavenly power which brings people back to life and redeems their souls. We are fighting over who will be saved among us, but this fight only leads to hatred and mutual insults.

"The salvation of people is a great thing. This is what makes Christianity different from other religions. Its purpose is the renewal and salvation of people. We name Christ our Savior, our Redeemer. But do we understand what dangers is Christianity saving us from?

"Does anyone know what the words 'Save yourself!' mean? It means that, during a fire, if you do not escape it, you will burn and die. There can be no debating here. Christianity, however, has been crying for nineteen centuries: 'Save yourself!' and mankind still has not moved from its place. It is impassively listening to all the calls of salvation, continuously thinking what does salvation mean. When people hear the words 'Save yourselves!' nobody thinks to jump, to run, to escape...

"Why is that? Because nobody knows what exactly must they save themselves from. And if someone claims he knows what the danger is but he, himself, doesn't run away from it, it means that the danger is not serious enough. Isn't that so?

"It is exactly like such. Even if we know from the Scriptures that only Christianity can save us from sin, curse, and death, do we truly understand what does Christianity saves us from? If we did, we wouldn't be speaking about it with such high spirits. When a man suffers, he doesn't care about the definition of benevolence nor of reflection but hurries to get rid of the pain.

"Nobody complains, screams, or hurries to get rid of the sin. Because of sin, man must repent, cry himself, sigh and look for forgiveness. But then he sins again. What does this mean? It means that, according to people, sin is the 'forbidden fruit' that seduces the man, giving him pleasure and sometimes, even a burning voluptuousness...

"The one who still believes in the existence of God has qualms of conscience after committing the sin, for the Lord hates the sin. But someone who does not care whether God exists or not, sins without any regrets, for he considers it to be normal. The first one feels the guilt, however, he is too weak to try and save himself; the latter feels no remorse at all. And so, the sin continues to survive in this world, while the cry of Christianity to save ourselves remains fruitless.

"Do we acknowledge what is God's curse from which Christianity can save us? Because of this curse, we learn His punishments for our sins, the most terrible one representing hell. If indeed, any sinful deed would be followed by immediate punishment, nobody would sin again. It is said 'Honor your father and mother...' If someone dared to offend their mother and would have his tongue immediately cut off, he wouldn't even dare to insult his parent again. In reality, something as such never truly happens.

"Mockery continues to flourish. Nobody feels the shame of the sin anymore, not even those who, instead of going to church on Sundays, go to the theatre, to the circus or even to the whorehouse.

195

Rather, the one who brazenly and impudently longs after someone else's money and wife lives better than the honest, disinterested people, who live miserably because they chose to listen to the qualms of their conscience.

"This correlation between sin and punishment is kept hidden from our minds and, but it is explained by the teachings of the afterlife. These teachings undoubtedly say that sinners will indeed be punished, but only in the afterlife. Also then, the righteous ones will be rewarded. But people live now, in this life, not the afterlife. Firstly, the afterlife is doubted by many, and secondly, even those who believe in the afterlife have developed such a poor concept around it that they favor a comfortable life on earth instead of the happiness in heaven.

In conclusion, nobody is afraid of God's punishment nowadays. With regards to hell, even if it sounds scary in an ideational way, nobody seems to rush and save himself from it...

"We continue to claim that only Christianity can save us from death. Nobody doubts the existence of death. Everybody fears it and wishes to escape it, including the suicidal people who would refuse to take their lives if someone would take their pain away and create them honorable conditions for a decent life. But the problem is that, indiscriminately, all Christians die, and there hasn't been one single case of someone who didn't. Theology can explain this discrepancy between the Christian teaching of overcoming death and what we actually see in reality. This teaching refers to what is sure to come. Yes,

Christians will die, but God will resurrect them and they shall live until the ages of ages.

Again, we talk of a future whose existence is doubted by too many. We can only believe in such a future. People want to escape death but they haven't yet seen any model worth following. The Resurrection that is yet to come leaves such a large room for disputes and different interpretations that it makes it impossible to reach a common conclusion in the near future.

"If we would observe our daily lives, we would notice that there are things we can simply ignore and things that we have to do – because their completion is mandatory. For example, we can or we cannot go to the theatre, follow fashion, or respect the behavior conduct. But we cannot break the law of equilibrium while walking, otherwise, we'll slip and injure ourselves. We can show indifference towards laws established by men, but we cannot disregard the laws established by God. If a person acknowledges and respects these laws— he receives a benefit, and if not— he receives a prejudice. If a person is in suffering, it means he broke a law. For instance, if he breaks the law of equilibrium, he will fall.

"All of us experience suffering and worries. Life has become unbearable for many. This happened because we defied Christianity. But we cannot deal with our own mistakes because we maintain distorted ideas about sin, punishment, hell, and death. People think of sin as something tempting despite being extremely damaging. We don't see God's punishments for what they are either. We see His judgment as an earthly one, ending either in exempt or condemnation.

We forget that God's Judgment had begun with the moment when the Light descended into the world.

"People ignore that God means unimaginable mercy and endless love. God punishes no one. Nevertheless... Punishments exist and they exist here, in this life...

"God's punishments are the fatal consequences of trespassing the laws established by Him. They are the physical and spiritual sufferings that sin produces in man; everything that makes his life unhappy, difficult and painful. Hell is also our current life, with all its shortcomings, with all the sufferings; the nostalgia, the tears, the pains and the struggles.

"Hell is the suffocating social life, the family life from whom Leo Tolstoy partially lifted the curtains in *The Kreutzer Sonata.*

"Hell is the meaningless and boring job, the useless information, the fruitless work, everything that transforms us into miserable people, trapped into little boxes.

"Hell is the lack of a piece of bread, the begging out of necessity, the body, and spiritual hunger.

"Hell is the feeble, inconsolable, helpless old age that utterly crushes a man's intellect and will, and stultifies his senses, bringing him to a second childhood.

"Hell is the unfruitful, barren wasteland, the springs swarming with deadly bacteria, the stench, the fetid swamps, the waste pits, the toxic climate, the noxious emanations...

"We are all in hell already. Listen to one's life and you'll hear the crying and the gnashing of the teeth. Can you find at least one man who is and has always been joyful, strong, healthy and prosperous, and who'll remain like that until his death?

"We will find many people satisfied, fortunate and apparently happy. Don't believe in such happiness. These are either under the effect of chloroform or hypnosis. The sick from the surgery rooms under anesthesia do not feel pain, cannot see other patients nor the doctor's scalpel cutting their body. Also, the ones barricaded from the agonies of hell with the commodities of this life think they are happy, but their first failure, their first serious illness, or the unavoidable old age sneaking unsuspectedly, instantly throw them into agonizing pains, ending their false happiness. And they don't even suspect they've already entered hell. This is the hell, where both believers and non-believers are currently living, that Christianity saves us from.

"The misinterpretation of death has created a big confusion. It is the first reason for this numb attitude towards Christianity that we see in the world. *Christ is Risen from the dead trampling down death by death... We celebrate the destruction of death...* This is how Christian hymns sound like. Death mockingly mows more and more people while Christians remain silent at the hearing of its roar... Today, the hymns for which people were burnt on pyres in ancient times are sung by talented singers and Christians admire not the profound meaning of the words, but the beauty of the music...

"People think there is only one type of death in the world and the same for everybody. But, in fact, there are two deaths or, more precisely, two

199

expressions of death; the natural death which certain people experience, and the unnatural death which the great majority of us die of.

"The death that we see every day– initially starts from diseases which retains our bodies in bed, accompanied by the pain and agony of dying. The death in agony deprives the man of his judgment and makes him wait the last moment of his life in fear. It represents the death that transfigures the human body into a stinking corpse – this death is unnatural, abnormal, unjust, and ugly, for it should not have been in the world. This death is misunderstood and seen as a universal regularity of nature, that represents the decomposition of the whole in its components, or the passing of the being from one form to another, from the material life to the immaterial one.

200

But the truth is that death should be absolutely painless and not accompanied by any suffering. By following the example of the saints, the man dies in full awareness, fearless, clearly sensing the end approaching, and is not afraid, but on the contrary, he rejoices; he senses the sweet feeling of drowsiness, that usually accompanies a long day of work, luring him to sleep. The decomposition of the body after this type of death is entirely different. If unnatural death comes with a heavy and ugly stench, shortly transforming the corpse into a fetid matter swarming with worms, in a natural death, these particularities are totally absent. No cadaverous stains appear on the body, no heavy smell, but on the contrary, a pleasant odor can sometimes be sensed. The decomposing process can sometimes take several hundreds of years[30].

"The unnatural death of man can be compared to the unripe grain of wheat. The grain of wheat tightly sticks to the bark. If the grain of wheat would feel with human senses, it would experience everything a man experiences when his soul separates from his body during the unnatural death. The natural death resembles the painless peeling of a fully ripe grain, which gladly rushes to bury itself in the ground.

"Christ destroyed this unnatural death, the source of all human agonies in the afterlife. Christianity calls mankind to save itself from this unnatural death, and indeed, it gives them the possibility to experience natural death, painlessly passing from one form of existence to another.

"With the power of our Lord Jesus Christ, people are being saved from sin, curse, and death. We believe that hierarchy contains this power but we argue which hierarchy truly holds the Grace: The Orthodox or the Starover. Let us solve this conflict the same way we've solved the debate between the two carpenters. Now we know what does Christianity save mankind from. Therefore, go and save people. If you succeed in doing this, it means that your hierarchy has the Grace too and that you have the power of God as well. And if you prove that you can do this, then nothing is left for us than to reach out our hands to each other and, together, eagerly continue the great work of revival and renewal of man. But if you cannot do

---

30 Hundreds of years – An exaggerated affirmation. The corpses of many saints have rotten. Some of the saints even prayed so that their bodies will rot after their death in order to not be worshiped by believers.

that and you witness how the people are saved in our Orthodox Church, then do not be stubborn and join us. So starting from today, I declare the missionary discussions closed for the reason that they failed to reach their purpose and all they did was to arouse the vain passion of discord..."

There are words in every language that name objects that are no longer in use. People don't renounce to use such words but instead, they keep them in their vocabulary as a heritage of past generations. Unable to see the object previously named with such words, people would imagine it by making assumptions or suppositions and, depending on the manner in which the object had been restored, they would assign different meanings to the word.

But by searching the dust of the archaeological excavations, they accidentally find the object, stare at it confused then involuntarily admit: 'Oh, so this is how it actually looks like, even though I was imagining it to be like...' So people find it unusual that they imagined the object to be different.

In a similar bewilderment was the audience of the missionary disputes now standing. Vladika had long finished his speech but the silence was still dominating the hall. Nobody moved nor made any sound. The same thought was present in everybody's mind: 'Oh, so this is what it was all about... and we were thinking that...' And all those who were thinking about it tried to elucidate their own thoughts, asking themselves how could they be able to think differently once and for all.

The former inmates from the asylum were the only ones not thinking about it. What was so enigmatic for others, it was crystal clear for them. Vladika had briefly told them about what they had already known for a long time. He called the Old Believers to go on the path that the inmates from the asylum had already gone. They had escaped from hell, and although the sin hadn't been entirely destroyed within them, they felt that its power had diminished and the darkness scattered, revealing what was from before. Their souls were filled with joy and they wanted to share this joy with everybody around.

Father Gherasim and Father Paul felt the disposition of their parishioners who gathered around the priests, forming a single heart and a single soul. And this soul was overwhelmed with a passion that burst out like a river from its bed, spreading a sea of sounds across the hall.

203

"Preide seni zahonnaia[31]..." they were singing the hymn in the old church in melodic style.

The voices were getting louder and louder and, in the rhythm of the music, they puffed their chests higher which caused their eyes to glow and their faces to brighten. They were confidently chanting about the Grace that had come, and indeed, the Grace did come to them. The public was staring at these people in amazement. The same thought continued to persist inside their minds: 'Oh, so this is what's all about...'

The voices were flowing and spreading everywhere, filling the hall and escaping through the windows outside, then boldly colliding

---

31 Preide seni zahonnaia – *The Shadow of the Law passed when Grace came...*

with the restless noise of people's cries in the streets. The passers-by stopped and listened to the melody of these born-again people, trying to capture its meaning; they were hearing something familiar in it, something close to their heart. Their souls were filled with an inexplicable sadness and nostalgia of something lost and long forgotten...

"Is Vladika closing the disputes?! How is it possible?" the troubled missionary asked his teacher who was about to exit the hall.

"Vladika has crossed the line," said the professor irritated. "This is an abuse of authorized powers! The Holy Synod will want to hear about this."

XVIII

he town was sleeping its morning slumber. The darkness had been chased away by the pale light of the morning. In the streets, electricity had already been turned off, but a lonely candle-light kept glowing in the window of the Archbishop's house. It was coming from Vladika's office.

After being all day in the middle of people, Vladika had only managed to snatch a few hours in the night to meditate. He analyzed the day that passed, gathering his thoughts that had dissipated in many directions during the day and placing them under a thorough inspection.

All this time, he rushed to check his private daily correspondence. But the meditation hours weren't silent all the time.

Many years of his episcopal service had passed in the new eparchy. During this time, he had managed to do countless great things, lots of which were already showing their results. But evil had not been resting. Recognizing a strong enemy in the person of the Archbishop, evil armed itself with all the available weapons, unceasingly splattering big globs of mud at him.

One of these globs, in the shape of a piece of paper with a very small handwriting, was now lying on the desk in front of the Archbishop's eyes. Next to it, a warning letter:

Your Grace! With profound sorrow must I inform about the inconveniences that have been prepared for you. Evil doesn't sleep... The complaint had been forwarded to the Synod. I'm sending you the rough draft that accidentally fell into my hands in order for you to have the possibility of preparing a worthy answer. Just in case...

A well-wisher

The venomous paper had been read by the Archbishop several times. His heart was in pain but his face, however, remained calm. He dived deep into his thoughts.

The denunciation contained detailed but distorted deeds that Vladika did during his service in the eparchy. It spoke about the fragility of the clergy, about the moral degradation of his sermons. Additionally, his concepts of Christianity were wrongly described. In conclusion, the author of the denouncement ended his letter by pleading the Synod to save their eparchy from this *wolf dressed in sheep clothing.* The signature read: *A zealot of Orthodoxy.*

"Yes, it would have been unusual if evil had kept silent... The father of lies has not been imprisoned forever yet, and as long as he roams loose, the sons of righteousness will be persecuted. Our Teacher warned us of such things. Persecutions do not frighten me. They have never intimidated anyone of those who've fought for righteousness for as long as the enemy kept his true form. It is difficult, however, to fight the devil when he takes the shape of an Angel of Light. Some of the Orthodox fighters are intimidated if the enemy's flag bears the inscription *Orthodoxy*. Their voices become silent and they drop their weapons, abandoning the fight...

"We have, however, the opportunity to win the battle. The work of Christ is the redemption and renewal of man. And if you, warrior of the Truth, see that the people around you are indeed renewing, perfecting, getting healthier in body, soul, and spirit, and becoming better individuals in general— know that you are on the side of the Truth. So then fight boldly with the enemy, even if he stands tall in front of you, performing great miracles and predictions.

"So the battle must be carried on restlessly. The voices of the earth continuously call for man to return to the underworld. The earth once served as a cradle for man, but for the mankind that grew up, it became a comfortable stratum, towards which he sometimes turns not for a curative, relaxing sleep, but for a careless dozing. And many continue to sleep, falling more and more comfortably into the deepness of ignorance. They sleep from dusk to dawn and from dawn to dusk. You need to constantly keep them awake and not be frightened if one of them, asleep, threatens you or if a stench will emerge from shaking his corpse...

"The true Church must lead people to eternal life. There never has nor will ever be such an establishment on earth of which can be said: This is the Kingdom of God on earth! So, good people, stop your sinful ways...' Bishops and Archbishops must, therefore, unceasingly wake mankind.

"And God forbid the land where the voices of protest will be silent!"

Made in the USA
Coppell, TX
03 August 2021